THE KING WHO CAME BACK

Fred Markham

THE KING WHO CAME BACK

FRED MacISAAC

COVER BY

PAUL STAHR

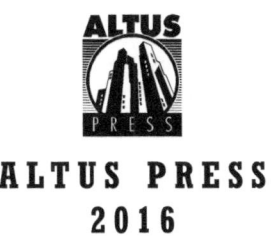

ALTUS PRESS
2016

© 2016 Steeger Properties, LLC, under license to Altus Press • First Edition—2016

EDITED AND DESIGNED BY
Matthew Moring

PUBLISHING HISTORY
"The King Who Came Back" originally appeared in the October 24 and 31, and
    November 7, 14, 21, and 28, 1931 issues of *Argosy* magazine (Vol. 224, No. 6–
    Vol. 225, No. 5). Copyright © 1931 by The Frank A. Munsey Company.
    Copyright renewed © 1958, 1959 and assigned to Steeger Properties, LLC. All
    rights reserved.
"About the Author" originally appeared in the February 15, 1930 issue of *Argosy*
    magazine (Vol. 210 No. 2). Copyright © 1930 by The Frank A. Munsey
    Company. Copyright renewed © 1957 and assigned to Steeger Properties, LLC.
    All rights reserved.

THANKS TO
Everard P. Digges LaTouche and Gerd Pircher

ISBN
978-1-61827-230-0

Visit *altuspress.com* for more books like this.
Printed in the United States of America.

TABLE OF CONTENTS

CHAPTER I

BAD WEATHER FOR KINGS

CRASH! RAT A tat tat! Boom!

"One can hardly hear himself think," observed the king.

"Rifles and machine guns," the prime minister said grimly. "That will put the fear of God in them."

"I wonder," the king shrugged. "Gentlemen, the council is in session."

He pulled out a chair, the high back of which was surmounted by a crown, seated himself and graciously indicated that the six dignified, elderly and brilliantly uniformed councilors should be seated. His majesty, himself, wore a suit of gray tweeds and was thirty years younger than his youngest adviser.

"Count Valdez," he said, "kindly explain to us exactly what the situation might be."

The prime minister made to rise, but dropped back in his chair when the king made a kindly gesture. He was a very fat, very florid, apoplectic old gentleman with a bristling gray mustache and fierce black eyes.

"The situation," he said, "is well in hand."

The king smiled. His smile was very attractive, gleaming white teeth beneath a tiny black mustache.

"Judging by the uproar," he said, "I question that."

"I mean," said the prime minister, "that the garrison of the city is loyal and will sweep the streets clear of mobs by nightfall."

"And outside the capital?" demanded the ruler.

The prime minister's face darkened. "The army in the north has mutinied, slain some of its officers and elected republicans to lead it. It is fraternizing with the common people. On the other hand, I'll stake my head on the loyalty of the army in the south. And, foreseeing some such contingency as the present, I was careful to bring into this city several of our most faithful regiments."

"And what is the state of mind of my people here in the capital?"

"Well, sire, they are disaffected, but we can hold them in check."

"My Lord Duke of Burzio," said the king, "what is your opinion?"

"That the situation cannot well be more serious," replied the duke, who was lord of the treasury. "We have very little money and we cannot sustain a civil war. While my confrere is correct in assuming that we can suppress rioting in the capital, I have information which indicates that not all the troops in the southern provinces are faithful to the crown. The North is united in demanding a republic. We have lost the army divisions quartered there and General Torres is a traitor. He will undoubtedly command the Northern Republican army which, reenforced by the National Guard and the militia of that part of the kingdom, will be ready in a few weeks to invest the capital.

"Of course your majesty will put himself at the head of his troops—"

"A moment, please. Gentlemen, how strong is republican sentiment? Frankness is requested."

"It's the world depression, sire," said Count Turino, minister of foreign affairs. "Our peasants are hungry and they listen to demagogues. They feel that the crown has failed them. They do not know what a republic is, but they want it. And the inhabitants of the cities are equally disaffected."

"With the unfortunate high percentage of illiteracy," remarked the king, "they are incapable of governing themselves."

The "porter" took aim at the king.

"They wouldn't get the chance," the minister replied. "There are a dozen scoundrels of good family, including some high military officers in the conspiracy to take advantage of conditions and overthrow our government. They will give the nation an oligarchy under the guise of a republic. Well, we'll fight to the death."

The fire of a battery of machine guns almost under the palace walls rattled the window frames of the ancient residence of kings.

"While we are talking, people are dying out there," said his majesty dolefully. "There seems to be little doubt that there will be a general rising throughout the kingdom in favor of a republic when the Northern rebels move south."

"Unfortunately, sire, yes."

"But we can muster a strong army, no doubt, and, with good leadership, hold our own?"

"Yes, sire, certainly, sire," asserted the various councilors.

The king brought his fist down with a crash upon the table.

"I'll have none of it!" he declared. "I don't want my kingdom torn by civil war. I don't want to hold my throne by slaughtering hundreds of thousands of my misguided subjects. The days when a king regarded his people as pawns whose life or death was of no consequence are gone, gentlemen."

"Then what does your majesty propose to do?" asked the prime minister sourly.

"I believe that the character of the population of this nation demands a monarch. Republics are only successful among very enlightened races and, while I have done all that a king could do in a dozen years to further the progress of education, the fact remains that my subjects are benighted. That is why I struck with an iron hand two years ago, shot down the rebels in the West mountains and executed the ringleaders of the uprising. I will not permit a few willful men to overthrow a good and stable government—"

"Hear! Hear!" the faithful courtiers applauded.

"But a government cannot maintain itself in defiance of the will of the great majority of the people, however misguided. I do not want the foot of my throne covered with blood. I do not propose to lead an army from one end of the land to the other over the bodies of multitudes of my subjects. What you gentlemen tell me confirms my own observations. There is a nationwide demand for a republic. Let them have it. I will abdicate."

His statement threw the council into consternation. These members of the ancient nobility saw their own privileges falling with the throne. Besides, they were imbued with fanatical loyalty to the royal house. They pleaded with him, implored him, wept and stormed without affecting him in the least.

"A month ago," he said, smiling ironically, "you held a meeting to request me to marry and provide an heir to the throne. There is no longer such a necessity. Count Valdez, draw up a form of abdication. I will sign it immediately."

"Hear me, sire," pleaded the old grandee earnestly. "The instant you sign, our soldiers, without, will throw down their arms and a mob will storm the palace. You are signing your death warrant."

"No," replied the king. "I think my people will be grateful to me for saving them from the horrors of a civil war. I shall be a popular idol."

THE DUKE DE BURZIO, dark, saturnine, hollow-eyed and devoted, dared to lay his hand upon the sheet of paper.

"Your majesty appears to believe that this is a spontaneous outburst of the people," he said. "It is an ingeniously fomented revolt and firmly in the hands of a band of unscrupulous scoundrels. They are fully aware that the establishment of a republic will not put bread in the mouths of the poor. They are aware that, in a couple of months, things will have gone from bad to worse and there may be a popular movement for your recall. Remember that you are the sole survivor of the house of Aronhof, which once ruled over most of Europe.

"You have not a living relative. You are a bachelor. When you die there is no one with a legitimate claim to our throne. Do you suppose these rogues will permit you to abdicate peacefully? Do you suppose you can retire to your estates to live comfortably until you are recalled to the throne? Czar Nicholas abdicated. What became of him? And remember Louis XVI and Charles I of England!"

The king nodded, much impressed. "And your suggestion is—"

"Mount your horse. Take sword in hand. Lead forth your faithful legions; rely upon your loyal generals. Though outnumbered, your case is not hopeless."

"The civil war again," the young king said sternly. "Years of it. Modern warfare with its horrors. Gas, big guns, bombs, the famines and pestilence which would follow. Sorry, my lord duke. I am a king with a conscience. They want a republic. I don't think it will be good for them, but I have no intention of ruining my country and being responsible for a million deaths to prevent it. I am afraid I could not sleep nights thinking about murdered women and babies. I have been horribly distressed by the killings during these two days of rioting. I'm going to abdicate and take my chances."

"You will be torn to pieces by an insane mob, sire," warned the prime minister. "They have been hanging you and burning you in effigy for two days in the city."

"You will make my abdication public in two hours," commanded the king.

He drew the sheet of paper toward him, dated it, wrote three words: "I hereby abdicate," signed it and rose from the table.

"Gentlemen," he said, "I thank you for your loyalty. Do what you can in your own interests. Good morning."

He left the room, heedless of their protests, and strode to his apartment. From one of his windows he looked down upon the public square. A regiment of steel-helmeted and breastplated cuirassiers was drawn up at the left. In the center was a battery of French 75's, at the right a regiment of foot guards. Lying motionless on the far side of the square were a score of still forms. From windows of houses opposite, rioters were sniping at the king's troops.

"It's a pity," he said aloud. He turned to a cabinet, took from it some ornaments, rings and jeweled decorations whose importance to him far overshadowed their intrinsic value of fifty thousand or so. Opening a drawer of his desk, he removed a packet of a few thousands in bank notes, thrust them into his wallet, went to a closet and put on a cloth cap, looked around the richly furnished apartment in which ten generations of Aronhofs had lived and died, sighed and left the room.

FIVE minutes later he came out of a grove in the royal park and crossed a wide, closely cropped and level field toward a row of long, low buildings on the far side. A soldier who came running toward him with bayonet fixed, straightened up suddenly and saluted smartly. The king was a familiar figure about the airport, where he was very well liked by the flyers for his democratic ways.

King Carlos nodded, and continued on his way. Seeing a

door of one of the hangars open, he entered and discovered a young man in civilian clothes who was watching a mechanic work on a small monoplane.

"Hello, Jervis," said the King of Berania in perfect English. "Going somewhere?"

The young American whirled. "Your majesty!" he ejaculated. "This is a surprise. I've just come down from Paris with dispatches for our embassy."

"Will you do me a great favor?" requested the monarch. "Load up your bus and lift me across any one of our frontiers."

Will Jervis gaped at him in astonishment.

"I don't understand, sir."

His majesty smiled bitterly. "I'm out of what you have, on several occasions, so amusingly called 'the king business,'" he said. "My abdication has not been announced, but it will be in two hours. I don't think my life will be worth much after that."

"I was supposed to report at the embassy, but I'll take a chance and send a messenger with the dispatches. I'll be ready in ten minutes, sir."

"I knew I could rely upon you," said the king. "I expected to have to make a personal appeal to one of my own officers, but loyalty appears to be at a premium in Berania nowadays."

"Best get into the bus and put on a cap and goggles, sir. I'll have to call in the royal mechanics—"

"Who, in all probability, are one hundred per cent republicans."

The king climbed into the aëroplane and Jervis sent the man who had been inspecting his machine in search of help. He climbed in beside the king and the pair sat silent while the tanks were filled and the various preparations for a flight were made.

"We'll have to go north, of course," said Jervis. "Too risky flying over the sea."

"I am in your hands," replied the abdicated monarch.

All was ready. The propeller was spun, the engine roared, the monoplane ran out of the hangar, taxied across the field and took the air. For a time there was a speck in the sky and then it vanished. And that was how King Carlos of Berania left his kingdom.

CHAPTER II

A FRIEND IN NEED

THE DISAPPEARANCE OF the ruler of Berania threw a pall over the triumph of the republicans of that nation. His abdication was received with wild joy by the republican masses who ran riot through the streets of the capital, Madrova, for a week, unchecked by their leaders; who robbed and looted and drank and reveled to their hearts' content.

But there was gloom in the hearts of the revolutionary junta that moved immediately into the palace and set about taking over the government. Carlos had played them a scurvy trick. They had hoped for two things; that he would take the field against them and thus establish himself as an enemy of the people, or that he would abdicate and surrender himself into their hands, whereupon they would try him for high crimes and misdemeanors and cut off his head.

The cutting off of the head of Carlos would end royalist hopes forever, as he was the last of the Aronhof line, and, as the Aronhofs had ruled Berania for five hundred years, there was no other family with the most remote claim to the throne.

In their wrath, they imprisoned the members of the privy council and the close friends and adherents of the king and then, after a conference, announced to the world that King Carlos was a thief and absconder; that he had carried off the crown jewels of Berania and for years had been looting the treasury and had invested fifty millions of dollars in England and America.

Naturally this information provoked a storm of execration among the people of Berania and gave the new government an excuse to plead poverty and therefore inability to improve immediately the condition of the common people. Its next action was to put a price of one hundred thousand dollars upon the head of the absconding monarch and to ask neighboring nations' permission to extradite him as a common thief.

And it filled Carlos Aronhof and Will Jervis, in their rooms in a small hotel in a quiet quarter of Paris, with indignation and dismay.

Carlos was a modern, up-to-date king. He was young, not quite thirty-one. He had been orphaned by a bomb which killed his father and mother when he was thirteen years old and he had thrown aside the regency and ascended the throne at eighteen to prevent his country from plunging into the World War. For four years he had kept Berania out of the war to her great profit, though the diplomats of both sides schemed and conspired to secure his assistance.

Ruler of a great and ancient kingdom, he had observed with distress that his people were backward and burdened by illiteracy. And he had not scrupled to spend vast sums in the cause of education. He was well-read, alert, keen-minded, generous and firm and the best king that Berania had ever possessed.

A racial characteristic of his family was a pendulous under lip and no chin. In Carlos the under lip was full, but not pendulous and the chin was strong. Perhaps it was because his mother had been an English princess that the bad blood of the Aronhofs had been tempered.

He had been immensely popular during the fat years that followed the war and he had seen his popularity wane with consciousness that world conditions alone were responsible.

His refusal to marry a princess whom he did not love had been a cause of great grief to his adherents, who did not fail to point out to him that he had no brothers or sisters or cousins to succeed him. Of course he expected to make a state marriage in time but, like the Prince of Wales, he could not bring himself to wed one of the few available princesses. And now that unpleasant duty was eliminated.

Will Jervis had been presented to him by the American ambassador upon his appointment as an under-secretary at the American legation two years before. Jervis was about his own age and very much his type, and the fact that he was an American interested the king particularly. Carlos had always hoped to visit America, but conditions in Berania made it more imperative each year that he keep his hand on the throttle. He had had many talks with Jervis about the land across the Atlantic and he told him, laughingly, when they landed at Le Bourget Field near Paris that at last his opportunity had come.

"I think I would like to live in America," he said.

"You may visit the country for six months and probably get your permit extended another six months, but you can't live there," said the American, smiling, "because of the immigration restrictions. The Beranian quota is filled for a year ahead."

"Immigration!" cried the king in surprise. "Ah, I forget. I am now a private citizen."

"Your majesty can reside in England or France or Germany, of course."

"Yes," said the king dubiously. "But how shall I live?"

Jervis looked astonished.

"You haven't provided for that?"

Carlos shook his head. "I am not like your South American presidents. I have not stolen money from my country and placed it in banks abroad. I have taken what funds I had in my desk, about five thousand dollars in your money. Unless I am recalled, I am afraid I must earn my living, my friend."

"Good Lord!" exclaimed the American. "But you're a king! You can't work. The British government will make you an allowance. Your mother was one of their princesses."

"No, it smacks of charity."

"Well, they will be grateful to you for stepping down and they will probably pay you a pension."

"Not the men who are about to rule my misguided people," said the king with a sigh. "Anyhow, we can dine together in a good Paris café. Let us get a motor car and go to town. Do you think that you will be in trouble for assisting me?"

Jervis laughed. "If they find out I carried you off, and no doubt they will, they will probably protest to my chief who will have to dismiss me. I'm not dependent upon my salary and I'd sacrifice a lot more to help you."

They dined well that night and secured adjoining rooms at a quiet hotel. The king invited his rescuer to breakfast with him next morning and Jervis entered at nine with the morning newspapers.

"**A NICE** lot of rotters have moved into your palace, your majesty!" he exclaimed. "This is the most abominable thing I have ever heard of!"

He passed over the journals which the king perused in silence.

"The crown jewels," he said, after a minute, "are reposing in the strong room at Madrova Castle. It would take a four ton truck to transport them and they are worth fifty or sixty millions of your dollars. I shall immediately answer this abominable falsehood."

"Hold on a minute, sir. They are going to ask your extradition as a thief. England would not consent to it, but France might. The socialists are on top and they hate kings and there is a lot of latent rancor here because you wouldn't join France in the late war. Better get to England and issue your statement from London."

"You are right, Jervis." The king looked thoughtful. "This may be a plot to find out where I am staying. You understand that they won't rest while I am alive. The permanency of their republic depends upon the extinction of the line of Aronhof."

"We had to identify you at the landing field last night and

the French government already knows where you are. You can't very well hide a king. Do you really think they will try to assassinate you?"

"It's a political necessity. In six months, the republic having failed to improve living conditions, there will be a demand for my return."

"Well, the French government will protect you as a matter of course. I saw a couple of fellows lounging outside the hotel this morning who look like detectives."

"Unfortunately I am not a fatalist," said Carlos with a sigh. "I am young. I have been a king and have never had any fun. I would like to live and love and be happy. If I had an income I think I would pray for the success of their republic. Unfortunately I was trained to be a king, therefore, all I know is statecraft, for which there is no demand, and such menial trades as riding horses and driving a motor car."

The phone rang and Jervis answered it at once.

"A delegation bearing the distinguished consideration of the President of France is on its way," he reported.

His majesty sighed. "And I have not even a uniform to wear. Well, it does not matter."

"Will you excuse me, sir? I have a code telegram to send, explaining to the ambassador how I happen to be in Paris instead of Madrova."

"If ever I ascend my throne again—" began the king gratefully.

"Please, sir, don't take that attitude. I shall be grateful all my life that the chance to serve you was given me."

The king grasped his friend's hand with emotion. "There is one thing I can do," he said. "I have not abdicated as Grand Master of the Order of the Lion of Berania and I have in my possession the decoration of that order." From his wallet he drew the red and blue ribbon with the small golden lion and pinned it upon the breast of his friend.

"If it means anything to you," he said, "you are now a member of an organization which has never included an American or a commoner of any nation."

Jervis came to attention and saluted.

"I shall never deserve such a great distinction, your majesty," he said.

Carlos smiled sadly. "I doubt if any other member of the order is so worthy."

As Jervis spoke the telephone rang. As well as he could remember it was the first time that Carlos had even personally answered a phone call. Somebody had always taken it for him.

"Delegation from the Palais D'Orsay to present their respects to King Carlos of Berania," said the excited voice of the hotel manager.

"Let them come up," replied his majesty.

"I'll be going," stated Jervis, unpinning as he moved away the most sought after decoration in the world with the exception of the Order of the Garter, and carefully placing it in his breast pocket.

As he opened the door a man in the uniform of a hotel porter was standing there, in his hand, a gun. He raised the weapon, pointed it toward the king, but, before he could fire, Jervis had torn it from his grasp.

"The first attempt," said Carlos calmly. "Cover the brute until I can have the hotel officials take him into custody."

He stepped to the phone and asked the management to take charge of the would-be assassin. Jervis held the trembling wretch by the collar until three or four porters and waiters relieved him of his charge and whisked him away just as four Frenchmen in frock coats and high hats emerged from the elevator at the far end of the corridor.

His majesty, looking very soldierly and handsome though he wore gray tweeds, received the delegation cordially and the American marveled at the dignity of the dethroned monarch.

The spokesman of the French nation welcomed Carlos to France and expressed a hope that he would not remain very

long upon French soil because of the violent republican sentiment of a section of the population and because the Beranian
republic had already wired asking his extradition as an absconding public official.

"The President begs to suggest that you would be more happy
in England."

"Convey to the president expressions of my gratitude," replied
the king. "And assure him that I shall leave France almost immediately."

Much gratified, the delegation bowed itself out and the unfortunate monarch glanced whimsically at the American.

"To use an American expression," he said, "our French friends
wish to say, 'What's your hurry, here's your hat.'"

"It's damnable," declared Jervis.

"The British will admit me, give me a pension perhaps, fail
to protect me and I shall be dead in a week or two," stated
Carlos. "I wonder if there is any way for a king to disappear."

The young American looked thoughtful.

"You are one of the most photographed men in the world,"
he said slowly, "but something might be done along that line."

CHAPTER III

SNUG HARBOR

SIX MONTHS AFTER the abdication of King Carlos of Berania, Mrs. Mason Swasey of Beverly Hills, California, hired a new chauffeur. Mrs. Mason Swasey was a widow who lived grandly on a fifty-acre estate in the foothills. She owned a gigantic *hacienda* which had thirty rooms with baths and six rooms with two baths. She had a swimming pool one hundred and twenty feet long and thirty feet wide; a stable full of horses and a garage full of automobiles, the cheapest of which cost five thousand dollars. She was a portly, red-faced widow of fifty whose career could only be paralleled in fairy tales or in California.

A quarter of a century ago Mrs. Mason Swasey was married to a person named James M. Swasey, generally known as Shifty Jim, and they lived in a shack on a hill near Long Beach, California, which is about twenty miles south of Los Angeles. When his health was good, which was seldom, Shifty Jim earned money picking oranges, and Mrs. Swasey, whose health was always good, earned more by taking in washing. She had a mule and a tumbledown buggy which she drove a couple of times a week into Long Beach and picked up bundles of soiled clothing from various beach houses, took them back to the hilltop and washed them very clean. She was buxom, cheerful, ignorant, kindly and more or less contented.

In those days, when Los Angeles was a small city and Long Beach was a village, there were no such things as hot and cold

16

running water in such homes as were occupied by Mrs. Swasey, and she secured water in a bucket from a well, heated it upon a kerosene stove and made linen spotless, by using plenty of elbow grease. With all this, she had time to have two children, James and Gladys, who were toddlers when the earthquake occurred.

It was not much of an earthquake; not even enough of a shock to damage the shack, but the next time Mrs. Swasey lowered a bucket into the well it came up very dirty and smelling devilishly.

There was no question whatever that there was petroleum in Mrs. Swasey's bucket. In that remote period, nobody dreamed that there was oil in Southern California and, at first, Mrs, Swasey was furious because her well was polluted. She went to Long Beach and told her tale to a customer whose husband happened to be an engineer and he drove back with her in her buggy.

It was Mrs. Swasey's luck that he happened to be an honest engineer and one who knew oil when he saw it. He poked around the hill for a couple of days and then informed Mrs. Swasey that it looked very much to him as if she were living on top of a sea of oil.

Did she own the hill? She did. It had cost almost nothing and she had it almost paid for. He looked at her title and smiled to see that, while the original owners reserved mineral rights, they had not reserved oil rights. He went right up to Long Beach, formed a company, sunk a well and erected a derrick in Mrs. Swasey's back yard. He didn't have to go down very far before he was taking out more oil than he had storage accommodations.

IN THOSE remote days, the oil supply was limited, and professors were always announcing that, in no time at all, the nation's supply would be exhausted, especially if people kept burning it in those pesky horseless carriages. And it commanded a fancy price.

Jim Swasey heard about the oil and came back from the orange groves. Mrs. Swasey stopped taking in washing. People predicted that the Swasey oil supply would soon be exhausted, which shows how much people know, for, if you drive down to Long Beach from Los Angeles to-day, you will find ten thousand derricks rearing their unsightly heads skyward on Mrs. Swasey's hill and the surrounding country, and oil pouring out of the ground so fast that it is cheaper in some parts of Southern California than spring water.

You wouldn't believe how many millions of dollars poured in upon the astonished Swaseys. They became so rich that Shifty Jim drank himself to death in a couple of years. Mrs. Swasey was built of different metal. She moved into Los Angeles, bought herself a fine home on West Adams Street, hired fine dressmakers, tutors for her children, automobiles and everything that money could buy. And she broke into society in a big way.

To a certain extent Los Angeles got rich with her. Thousands of people became very wealthy through oil and most of them were just as ignorant and not nearly so level-headed as Mrs. Swasey. She went to work to improve herself. She studied, and in time spoke very good English, though she reverted to her washwoman vocabulary when she became angry.

She had had the Beverly Hills estate for five years when she crowned her career, though she did not know it at the time, by hiring, as a chauffeur, the dethroned King of Berania.

"**WHAT** a perfectly gorgeous man!" exclaimed Gladys Swasey when she saw her mother getting out of her Minerva with the assistance of a tall, slender, soldierly-looking person who had been driving the car.

The young man was clad in a blue suit which fitted him like a uniform. His hair was jet black, his complexion a romantic olive, his eyes large, lustrous and melancholy, his nose straight as a Greek idol's, his chin rather pointed and his mouth pleasant with an unusually full under lip.

Gladys Swasey was twenty-five years old and unmarried. She

was a magnificent example of what the climate of California, mingled with a too-hearty diet, can do for a young woman. She stood five feet eight, she weighed a hundred and forty-six pounds, she was massive without being fat, statuesque without being stodgy, beautiful as the Goddess of Liberty in New York Harbor is beautiful. And if you could see the legs of the Goddess of Liberty, they would probably look very much like those of Gladys Swasey. Solid, substantial, with swelling calves and ankles that were not thin. Gladys was blond.

She was super-intelligent, she had a hearty laugh, fine white teeth, and the complexion of a milkmaid.

She and her brother were going to inherit about a hundred millions of dollars and they felt their oats, as it were.

After aiding Mrs. Mason Swasey's bulk to solid ground, the new chauffeur drove the gleaming automobile around to the garage and Gladys pounced upon her mother.

"Where on earth did you get him?" she demanded. "He's adorable!"

Mrs. Mason Swasey looked through her glasses and down her prominent nose at her daughter.

"At an employment office," she said testily. "He's some kind of a foreigner. He knows how to drive all right. And I'd hate to have to fire a good man because my daughter started to make a fool of herself about him, especially when she's old enough to know better."

"Don't be a chump, mother," said Gladys, laughing. "I'm not the sort of heiress who elopes with chauffeurs. But, he is stunning! What nationality is he?"

"Well," stated Mrs. Swasey, "he says he's a Spaniard, but has lived most of his life in England. I'm giving him a hundred and fifty a month and chuck and a room over the garage with the other chauffeur, and I'm going to keep an eye on you. Where's Junior?"

"Out at the polo field, I suppose. Where else would he be?"

"Well, he might be getting into trouble with another of them motion picture actresses."

Gladys laughed appreciatively, passed her arm through that of her mother and went with her into the Swasey palace.

Carlos Aronhof ran his motor car neatly into the garage, descended from it and regarded it approvingly. He was very much at home with a Minerva, having formerly owned four of them, not to mention a fleet of Hispanos, some Renauds and a handful of Rolls-Royces.

He was glad he had secured a job in this lovely place at a hundred and fifty dollars a month. Carlos had been having a tough time since that day in Paris when the French government welcomed him and insinuated that he couldn't depart too soon for its satisfaction.

The republic survived in Berania; general living conditions were worse than they had been under the monarchy but there had been no rising of royalists to restore the monarchy. It didn't look as though there ever would be a return to the legitimate ruler.

Two weeks after the reception in Paris, Carlos Aronhof, bearing the name of Carl Decker, had landed in New York from the second cabin of the Bremen after a superficial examination by immigration officials.

Carl Decker had an American passport bearing a picture which didn't look in the least like him. Where he got it and how he got by with it is still a state secret, but there was sympathy in high quarters for the young king whose life was not safe in Europe, and apparently the skids were well greased. He got by without the slightest difficulty.

He lived for a few months in New York, doing nothing and keeping out of public places until all chatter over his whereabouts by European correspondents had died out. He had no illusion that he had permanently escaped assassins from Berania but, aided by Jervis, he had thrown them temporarily off the track.

He had shaved off his becoming black mustache and a barber on shipboard had eliminated all traces of his distinctive Beranian hair cut. And, at the end of two months, he was faced with the pressing necessity of earning his own living.

Carl had escaped from his native land with less loot than any monarch in history.

Yet the king had to get a job, and he didn't know how to do anything for which people earned money. While he was a highly intelligent, very brilliant man with a keen sense of humor, he had no trade, profession or gainful occupation and, in addition, was handicapped by Aronhof pride.

The Aronhofs had been rulers of great nations for a score of generations—mostly bad rulers—and their slightest wish had been law. While Carl took a modern, common sense view of "the king business," in which ducking bombs with nonchalance had been part of the job, he had been born and brought up in a stiff-necked court, trained to consider himself as God's "chosen, kotowed to by millions all his life and he couldn't shuffle that off in a few weeks or a few months.

Also, he had the European's senseless contempt for Americans, and he hated the idea of taking orders from any of them, so he procrastinated until he had only three thousand dollars left and then he read an advertisement.

A philanthropist would take your money and put it in a California oil company which would return you at least a hundred per cent profit in dividends inside of a year. Carl gave him twenty-five hundred dollars, and that was that.

However, it reminded him of California, a land of perpetual spring. The weather in New York was insufferable. With his last supply of cash he bought himself a ticket for Los Angeles, giving the name of John Parker, a name which he dropped after the tedious journey, feeling himself safe from any pursuit.

WHILE Los Angeles is the Mecca of ruined archdukes, and has been visited by a few British princes and nondescript Continentals who made princes of themselves while crossing the

Atlantic on a steamer, it had never had the pleasure of greeting a bona fide king, and would have made whoopee for Carlos if he had broadcasted his arrival.

But the ex-king of Berania was strictly incognito. He had been free from the attentions of the assassins for several months and he had no desire to inform them of his whereabouts. He took a room at a quiet hotel and went sight-seeing for a week or so, then, all of a sudden, he discovered he had no money.

For the first time he began reading the want ads. He answered advertisements of people who wanted him to sell lots in cemeteries and vacuum cleaners. He would have tried to get into the movies save that his face and figure on the screen would be equivalent to giving the enemy his address.

He got down to the point where he faced actual starvation, and then he presented himself at an employment office and offered himself as an expert chauffeur and mechanic on foreign cars. He was not lying. Carl was not only a marvelous motorist, but he could take down the engine of a Minerva or a Hispano and put it together so that it would work properly. Gas engines had been his hobby when he was king.

Mrs. Mason Swasey was a great lady, but she retained some of her old habits. One of these was personally selecting her servants. She saw King Carlos of Berania, was impressed by him and hired him. That was how he came to be in a garage in Beverly Hills.

"How are ye, Bill?" said a rough but friendly voice. Carl turned from his contemplation of the mechanical marvel and looked into the round red face of an Irishman in a chauffeur's livery which was not unlike that of the Royal Beranian Foot Guards.

"Carl is the name," he replied stiffly.

"Bill is a good name, too," grinned the man in uniform. "Tom Clancy, that's me. The old elephant told me to show you your hang-out."

"I'll be greatly obliged."

"I thought you was a wop but you're a cockney," Clancy charged.

"I am not, my man. I am a Latin, but I have spent much time in England."

"The hell with it."

"With what?"

"England. Come on, feller."

Carl followed him, with misgivings, up a flight of stairs, along a corridor and into a fine, bright, charmingly furnished chamber which contained a tiled bath and shower.

"You camp here," said Clancy.

Carl looked astonished. Servants in Berania didn't have such quarters. In fact, the king in Madrova was not more comfortably lodged, if much more ostentatiously. All of a sudden he smiled his brilliant smile, and his heart grew light.

Why not? He liked engines; he was in a remote corner of the world, absolutely unsuspected. He would have to drive that old woman and her big beautiful daughter around. No doubt the food would be good and the pay was sufficient. When the time came that Berania wanted her king back, he would slip away from Los Angeles, turn up in New York and no one would ever dream that he had been a servant.

"Not bad, eh?" demanded Clancy. "The madame says you're to go into Levy's on Wiltshire and get fitted to a uniform. You keep on the right side of her and you'll be sitting pretty. The girl is kind of nice, but the boy is a—" he used a contemptuous and very profane expression.

"Ah, the son! Mrs. Swasey told me she had a son about twenty-seven years old. A bad egg, eh?"

"Ain't been to bed sober as long as I've been here. You'll not have much to do with him. I'm the night driver, worse luck."

"Well, I'm greatly obliged to you, Mr. Clancy," said Carlos in a tone of dismissal.

"I'm going to take one of the small cars and run down to Hollywood. I been doing double duty since Schultz, the feller

whose place you're taking, got fired for swimming in the swimming pool."

"Indeed. Isn't that what it's for?"

"Not for servants. It costs about a hundred dollars on the
water meter to empty it and fill it, and the old elephant's tight
about water. She don't fill it any oftener than she has to so the
help is barred."

"But if they all have bathrooms, why aren't they as clean as
the family?"

"It's just the idea, Carl. So keep out of the pool."

The king, who had regarded it with approval upon his arrival,
shrugged his shoulders. "After what you say," he said, smiling,
"it can't be a very clean pool."

"You said something. Funny that people who have a hundred
million would be tight about a thing like that."

"A hundred millions! Are they that rich?"

"Richer."

That much money, he thought, was more than the annual
budget of the city of Madrova. In Los Angeles these people
seemed to have no special distinction. What a country!

CHAPTER IV

THE MAN IN THE THEATER LOGE

WILL JERVIS, SINCE his return to America, had lived in a small, comfortable apartment in New York's East Fifty-fourth Street. Technically he was under a cloud, as he had no business to carry off the King of Berania in his airplane, and the State Department had to drop him from the diplomatic service in order to preserve amicable relations with the new government of the Republic of Berania.

Actually, he had been a popular hero for a period of nine or ten days. The American people, confirmed democrats though they are, have always admired other people's kings and Carlos was the best-looking and most picturesque monarch who had survived the World War.

Thousands of editorials commended the young legation secretary for his achievement and he was compelled to listen to a speech from Mayor Walker and accept the keys of the city of New York upon landing in America. From Washington came an unofficial intimation that he would be welcomed back in the diplomatic service after things blew over. In the meantime he was content to live upon his ample income and amuse himself in the greatest city in the world.

He had received a letter from King Carlos shortly after the arrival of the ex-monarch in New York in which he was profusely thanked for the arrangements for Carl's admission incognito; then he heard no more. When he arrived home, about a month after Carlos, he expected to locate him and continue his good offices, but Carlos had dropped out of sight completely.

Jervis and Carlos Aronhof had not been intimate in Berania, but Will had come to appreciate the fine character of the ex-king during their flight and their days together in Paris and was eager to be of further service to him. However, he accepted the Aronhof's attitude without rancor.

Jervis thought he would have no trouble locating King Carlos in case of need, for the Federal authorities knew whom they were admitting under the name of Carl Decker and, undoubtedly, had a fatherly eye on him.

In this respect he was deceived, as he learned when lunching with an assistant Secretary of State at the Patroons' Club.

"Any notion what became of your friend the king?" asked Secretary Downes.

"No. Haven't you?"

"Not the slightest. We detailed a man to observe his movements and he kept track of him for a few months, but the fellow became careless and let Carlos move out of his hotel without trailing him. We haven't picked him up since."

Jervis laughed. "I thought your secret service was efficient."

"It is, ordinarily, but this was more or less a matter of form. The man wasn't a criminal and it wasn't likely that the Beranians would chase him across the Atlantic."

"Can't you find any man you want in the United States?"

"Don't be silly. Not even when we have their finger-prints. However, we're on the lookout for him and he will turn up."

"You are mistaken in thinking they won't pursue him to America."

"Why should they? The republic is firmly established."

"My dear fellow, the Beranians are about the most backward people in Western Europe. About seventy per cent of the population believes that kings rule by divine right and they don't know the meaning of the word republic. Carlos could land with a dozen men and have ten thousand in a couple of days and a hundred thousand in a week, just as Prince Charlie was able to raise Scotland in the eighteenth century though he landed there alone.

"The republic was brought about by a handful of politicians and disloyal officers of the army. It won't be secure while Carlos is alive, and, if he had any brothers or sisters or cousins, it wouldn't be safe then. When the Aronhof family is extinct there will be no one around whom the Beranian Royalists can rally."

"I see. Perhaps they have murdered him already."

"No, because the fact would have been made public. The gang in Madrova must convince the Beranians that the king is dead."

"If that's the situation, Carlos was a fool to abdicate. Why didn't he fight for his kingdom?"

"Because he happens to be a decent fellow and he didn't want to murder a portion of his population."

"You say he has no money?"

"I'm quite certain that he had only five thousand dollars when he escaped and he assured me that he had no hoard abroad. I believe he had a few valuable jewels. He could have easily come away with ample funds, but he didn't."

"Then he was a fool."

Jervis laughed. "No, just honest. So straight that he bends over backward. I'm rather worried about him, to tell the truth. It would be dreadful if the United States let him starve."

"**MAYBE** he'll go to work. Imagine a king digging in a ditch," said Dowries, laughing.

"I can imagine it," said Jervis seriously. "Carlos is so proud that he would prefer ditch digging to begging for his bread. Get the department busy, will you? I'd like to find him and help him if he needs help."

"Right. When I get back to Washington I'll ask the chief to send Yates after him. That fellow is the best detective drawing government pay. He'll find him. But we can't do anything for him. Imagine the howl from Congress if the President asked an appropriation to enable an exiled king to live in this country in idleness."

"Carlos wouldn't accept. The British Parliament would have voted him a pension, but he was too proud to live on bounty. That's one of the reasons he preferred to come to America."

"Well," said the secretary, "he's a good looking brute and a bachelor. All he has to do is to step on the auction block and sell himself to some heiress."

"I happen to know that Carlos remained unmarried because he would not make a state marriage. He wanted to love his wife, so that's out. Besides, the instant he proclaims his identity the assassins will come post haste from Berania."

"Well, maybe I'll have some news for you in a week or two," said the secretary. "What can we do for you? Would you like to be secretary of the legation in Cambodia?"

"I'm sitting pretty right here in New York. When you have a good post, let me know."

"We'll keep you in mind, Will."

UPON the evening of the day when King Carlos found shelter in the garage of Mrs. Mason Swasey, Will Jervis attended a musical comedy in a New York theater in the company of a certain Miss Muriel Waite. Miss Waite was dark, dashing, piquant and entertaining. She was a friend of several years' standing, their acquaintance having begun when she and her mother visited Madrova and were presented at court.

The curtain descended upon the first act and the lights in the auditorium flashed on. Womanlike, Muriel twisted her pretty head in all directions to discover whom she knew in the theater, gasped, clutched at Will's arm, and pointed excitedly.

"Oh, Will!'"she cried. "Look! In that second right hand loge. It's the King of Berania!"

Jervis followed her finger. Seated in a loge sat a handsome man of thirty years. He was dark, clean-shaven, with fine black eyes, the Aronhof nose, the Aronhof full under lip, and the fine soldierly figure of King Carlos. He wore full evening dress, a ruby stud in his shirt front—an idiosyncrasy of the king—and in the buttonhole of his coat lapel was a small rosette of gold and purple. Will Jervis had a right to wear that same rosette— it was notification that its owner was a member of the Order of the Lion of Berania.

"By George!" he exclaimed. "It's Carl, all right; but I'm hanged if I understand why he is on exhibition."

"He's going out," she said excitedly. "Come on, Will. He'll be awfully glad to see you."

"I doubt that, for he knows I am in New York and hasn't indicated the slightest desire to see me."

"Because a king can't go chasing people round. He expects you to find him. Come on."

She was standing and forcing him into the aisle. There was something in what she had said, he thought, and he was exceedingly curious to know why the king, who ought to be in hiding, was making a public display of himself.

They reached the lobby and observed the king standing just inside the outer door smoking a cigarette and talking to a tall, blond, handsome man, who had been seated with him in the loge.

"We'll walk right up to him," the girl declared. "Remind him that I was presented to him three years ago."

Carlos was looking directly at them as they approached, and his dark eyes gleamed with appreciation of the beauty of Miss Waite. His gaze turned on Jervis and dulled.

Will smiled brightly and awakened no answering smile. He turned away, forcing the charming girl to accompany him.

"What's the matter?" she demanded. "Why don't you go up and speak to him?"

"It is bad form to address a king. He must speak first. He cut me dead, my dear."

"But, my gosh, you saved his life, he will remember when you remind him."

"I have no intention of reminding him. I am not going near him."

"Then I am," declared the young woman; and she tore her arm from his restraining grasp and walked across the lobby to the distinguished pair.

"Of course you don't remember me, sir," she said with assumed diffidence, "but I was presented to your majesty in Madrova."

"Ah, my dear young lady," replied the ex-monarch, displaying gleaming white teeth, "I remember you perfectly, though I do not recall your name."

"Muriel Waite, sir."

"Ah, of course. But I am strictly incognito, you understand."

"I beg your pardon, then, for intruding."

"Not at all, Miss Waite. It is a pleasure. One finds exile dull, you know."

"I am with Will Jervis," she declared. "Naturally your majesty will remember him."

"But of course. I have not seen him."

His companion touched his arm and nodded toward Will, who stood a score of feet distant watching the scene with peculiar interest.

"I am eager to clasp his hand," said Carlos. "Ah, the bell for the next act! Please tell him, Miss Waite, to come to me at the next intermission."

He moved into the auditorium after dismissing the girl with kingly condescension. Aware that a score of people had been listening brazenly to their conversation, Muriel, with reddened cheeks, returned to her escort.

The house darkened and the operetta continues. When the lights went up for the second intermission, Jervis glanced at the loge. Empty. He frowned thoughtfully. His resemblance to Carlos was astonishing, but the fellow was a pretender, an impostor!

CHAPTER V

A SURPRISE ATTACK

THE THING WAS to be expected. The ex-king of Berania had disappeared from Paris, and rumor had it that he had come to America. The pickings for royalty in the United States were magnificent. Muriel Waite, for example, sweet, clever girl that she was, would marry Carlos in a minute and endow him with the millions which belonged to her. There were very few society girls of Jervis's acquaintance who wouldn't take a much less attractive man than Carlos for the privilege of being a queen, even an exiled queen.

As Carlos had refused to take advantage of his opportunities, an impostor had set up in his place. Of course, he would be too shrewd to claim that he was the ex-king of Berania. He would declare loudly that he wasn't, and thus he could not be apprehended for obtaining money under false pretenses.

On the other hand, he would show himself everywhere, counting upon his remarkable resemblance to the much-photographed king, and to deceive the sophisticated he wore the rosette of the Order of the Lion of Berania in his buttonhole. He had the good sense, however, to disappear from the theater as soon as he learned that Will Jervis was there.

If Will had not been trained in the diplomatic service he would have informed Muriel at once that her king was an actor; but being quite certain that she would not be given an opportunity to meet him again, since he would shun all acquaintances of the dangerous Jervis, Will said nothing and listened

31

Carl tore open the door of the tonneau.

to her lamentations at the disappearance of the monarch whom she had intended to invite immediately to her Long Island home.

If the apprehensions of the real Carlos were well founded, the impostor was taking a huge risk—not of going to jail, but of assassination. Possibly not, though. It would be natural for Carlos to overestimate the strength of royalist sentiment in Berania and assume that there was a chance of his recall. And, on the other hand, the Beranian murderers in search of the Aronhof were not likely to be deceived by an impostor.

Will had been near enough to hear the voice of the masquerader and knew that he spoke English with a very slight Latin accent. Carlos had no accent. The resemblance, however, was remarkable. It had deceived Will until the fellow smiled. His smile lacked the charm of Carlos's and his teeth were not so regular.

What to do about it? Nothing, for the moment. In the morning he might have an idea. No doubt the newspapers would carry stories about the appearance of the exile in New York. Of the people who had heard the conversation between Muriel Waite and the pretender there would be at least one who would tip off a reporter.

After the performance he led Miss Waite to a dancing place and at one thirty in the morning he took her home. She had chattered a lot about the poor but handsome monarch. Like most women, she was an ardent royalist. She pleaded with Jervis to get in touch with Carlos and induce him to weekend with the Waites. While Will liked Muriel, he was glad to be free of her.

HIS TAXI landed him at the entrance to his apartment house at ten minutes of two. He had to awaken the sleeping elevator operator to be transported to the sixth floor, said good night, inserted his key in his door and pushed it open.

A crack of light under the living room door surprised him, and he opened it. The room was brightly lighted, and a man in evening dress was seated in his most comfortable chair under a reading lamp, occupied with a magazine.

As Jervis entered, the man laid the periodical down, rose and bowed stiffly from the waist. The visitor had a long, dark face and an undershot jaw. He smiled courteously.

"How the hell did you get in here, and who are you?" demanded Jervis angrily.

"A thousand pardons, sir, for my intrusion," said the stranger. "I am Count Grandez, and I picked the lock."

"I don't know you, and I don't want to know you. Kindly get out."

The man extended both hands in an apologetic gesture. "In your position, my attitude would be the same," he said. His English was excellent, but his intonation betrayed his nationality.

"Beranian," ejaculated Jervis.

"Yes. As you yourself are a diplomat, you understand that a

gentleman may do, in the interests of the State, what he would not dream of doing for personal advantage."

"Well," replied Will, mollified, "I have tapped a few telephone wires myself in my day. Why not phone me and make an appointment instead of breaking into my home?"

"I have need of a secret interview, sir, which I trust that you will grant."

Jervis laughed. "Fire ahead," he said.

"You," said the visitor, "are a friend of Berania. You were the instrument of Carlos's escape. You are in touch with him at this moment."

"Your first two surmises are correct, the third is wrong. I am not in touch with him."

"Ah, but you know how to reach him."

"On the contrary, I have not seen nor heard from him since leaving Paris."

The Beranian smiled cajolingly. "I understand, of course, that his majesty dare not disclose his residence because of danger from the republicans."

"You, then, are not a republican."

The man looked indignant. "I am a gentleman, sir. I am loyal to the house of Aronhof. I wish to see my master and kiss his hand."

"Well, I'm afraid I can't help you."

"Permit me, sir, to explain the situation. We in Berania are ready to overthrow this cursed republic. We are working quietly but efficiently. Our party is large and growing, but we cannot act without word from his majesty. He must withdraw his act of abdication. He must return and take the field in person."

"My friend, King Carlos is prejudiced against civil wars. That's why he left his country. If there was a demand for his return by a united country, I presume he would agree to do so, but, if he had wished to take the field, he need not have left Berania."

"That, sir, was a grave error of which I shall convince him. You will kindly give me his address."

"Sorry. I haven't got it."

"Then to what address do you write him?"

"I do not write him."

"Do you expect me to believe that?" asked the man contemptuously.

"I don't give a hoot whether you believe it or not. I don't like your tone any more than I like your personality, I'll be obliged if you will clear out!"

THE MAN eyed Will shrewdly. "I happen to know you have seen him to-night," he said.

"You mean, doubtless, that masquerader at the Music Box," said Jervis indiscreetly.

"Ah," said the Beranian. "So you agree with me that that person was not King Carlos."

"Oh, he might have been," replied Jervis, quickly on guard. "I merely thought it unlikely that the king would show himself in that fashion. I did not get an opportunity to approach him."

"You knew he was not the king because you are in close touch with the king," persisted the visitor.

"I've said my say in that respect and I wish to go to bed. Good night."

"I am not leaving until you inform me where to find his majesty. I am able to enforce my demand." He clapped his hands. From Jervis's bedchamber came two men with drawn revolvers.

Jervis gazed at the new arrivals with astonishment and apprehension. He was in a bad fix. The armed men were bullet-headed, low-browed, dark-skinned individuals of a type with which he was familiar from residence in Berania. They would obey without hesitation any order of their leader.

"You remember, perhaps," said that person softly, "that

Berania was the last nation in Europe to abolish the State torture chamber."

Will Jervis was an unusually clear-headed, quick-thinking young man and while the man who called himself Count Grandez was speaking he had analyzed the situation in which he found himself and realized its extremely desperate nature.

He had grasped, immediately upon his indiscreet admission that he was not deceived by the pretender at the Music Box, that the address of the real King Carlos was only a secondary motive for this visit. Grandez was here to remove the chief peril to the success of the impersonation. The fellow at the Music Box was not an irresponsible opportunist. He had been set up by one faction or other in Berania for a purpose. Jervis was the only man in America who knew the king so well that he could not he imposed upon. Jervis, therefore, must be removed.

If, at the same time, they could force him to reveal the hiding place of the real Carlos, they would be pleased, but it was absolutely certain that they were here for murder. Will was unarmed. Grandez no doubt had a weapon and there were two revolvers on display.

Will was seated with his back to the bedroom. The gunmen had posted themselves like soldiers behind him. Grandez faced him, alert, in the big chair, behind which was a writing desk.

"If you are loyal to his majesty," Will said quietly, "I am sure you will find it difficult to explain to him that you tortured his friend to obtain his address."

"When one serves his country and his king," replied the Beranian, "he is justified in any action to further his purpose. I propose to drive little wedges of wood between your finger nails and the flesh. It is a simple form of torture, but the pain is excruciating."

"If I were convinced that you actually wish to serve the king," Jervis said slowly, "I might tell you what you want to know."

"You must take my word for it, Mr. Jervis."

"The king," Will said, "is in California. He is in a small town with a name you would not remember and at a hotel, the title of which is equally unpronounceable."

Grandez's face lit up with satisfaction.

"Write it down for me," he commanded. To reach the writing desk was Will's desire. He had said the king was in California simply because it was that part of the United States most distant from these scoundrels. He wished to reach the writing desk because it placed Grandez between him and his warriors and because, beside the desk, was a light switch that turned off the lights.

HE ROSE, walked past Grandez, who turned to keep an eye on him, pulled out the desk chair, touched the switch, which threw the room into darkness, and tackled Grandez around the waist and threw him to the floor.

An explosion split the air and a bullet whizzed past and embedded itself in the wall.

"Don't shoot, you fools!" screamed Grandez in his own tongue. "You'll hit me. Turn on the lights!"

Will had fallen on top of him. He had made a football tackle; his arms locked just below the man's hips, his head pressed against his groin. In the dark, Grandez swore Latin oaths and beat upon the top of the American's head with his fists, but the left hand of Will Jervis had found in the man's right hip pocket what he was seeking. He drew forth a small automatic, shifted it to his right hand and took aim.

His advantage over his three opponents was that he was thoroughly familiar with the room.

"Lights!" Grandez continued to bellow while he tried to get his hands behind his back and pinion the gun arm of his opponent. One of the men lunged toward the light switch. Knowing its exact location, Will fired in the dark. A howl of pain informed him that he had found a human target. Then the light went on.

It revealed the man who had pressed the button sliding to the floor, but the other desperado opened fire, regardless of the risk of hitting his chief. Will rolled quickly off the body of Grandez just as a piece of lead whined past and a few inches above him.

"Stop!" shrieked Grandez in his native tongue. *"Ah, Dios!"*

Jervis felt the man's form quiver as a bullet plunged into his soft flesh, then he dropped the marksman by planting two bullets from the automatic in his chest.

He sprang to his feet; too soon, for the wounded assassin on the floor beneath the light button had an uninjured gun arm. He fired, and his bullet hit Jervis in the thigh, inflicting a flesh wound; then Jervis ended the fight by drilling the man between the eyes.

The battle had lasted much less than a minute, but the entire apartment house was alarmed. Feet were heard running in the corridor, women were screaming in near-by apartments, and somebody was pounding lustily on the door.

Jervis glanced down at Grandez, who lay with his eyes closed, breathing heavily, and managed to limp to the outer door and throw it open. Then, faint and conscious of a terrific pain in his right thigh, he staggered to a chair and fell into it.

A man in pyjamas entered timidly and emitted a bellow of alarm when he saw three persons weltering in their blood upon the floor. A woman behind him fainted and was carried off by two men in the rear who also were in pyjamas. The night clerk of the apartment house thrust his way in.

"What has happened here?" he demanded. "Murder!"

"Get the police and a doctor. I think that one is alive," said Jervis faintly. "I'm wounded myself, but not seriously."

There was a doctor living upon the same floor who entered in night clothes, but with his kit.

"Robbers?" demanded the clerk of the half-fainting Jervis.

"I found the three of them here when I came home," Will explained. "We had a battle. Looks as though I won out."

"This man has a bullet in his left lung, but he will live," said the doctor. "Somebody call an ambulance. Are the others dead, Mr. Jervis?"

"I think so. Have a look at my thigh, will you?"

By the time the thigh was bandaged—the bullet had passed completely through the flesh and embedded itself in the floor—the police arrived.

Jervis was able to give them a brief statement before the doctor insisted that he be put to bed and a nurse installed. He allowed the surmise of the clerk to stand as likely to cause less sensation. In the interests of the King of Berania, the less published about his alleged supporters the better.

DURING the next ten days Jervis, flat on his back, read newspaper accounts of the movements of the ex-king of Berania with interest.

The man was registered at a fashionable hotel as Alfonso Gomez, and had insisted to visiting reporters that he was not King Carlos and was a Spaniard, not a Beranian; but he permitted himself to be photographed, and obviously he had no objection to being considered as the ex-monarch. He was seen about in public places, and in a few days was a regular visitor at night clubs in company with a celebrated blond show girl named Dora Doro. Will observed with concern, about six days after his accident, that Mr. Gomez had been a week-end guest at the Waite home on Long Island.

There were flowers and notes from Muriel, but he had had no opportunity to warn her regarding the impostor, and it appeared that the fellow was brazen enough to accept the invitation which she had probably mailed to the address which was given in the newspapers the day after his appearance at the Music Box.

On the tenth day Will received a letter bearing a Los Angeles postmark and written in a hand unknown to him. He opened it carelessly, but his astonishment at its contents was complete. It was from King Carlos.

My Very Dear Friend:

I was grieved to read in the newspapers that you were wounded in a battle with three robbers whom you discovered in your apartment. Am I right in surmising that they were not robbers, but agents of the government of my unhappy country?

I have refrained from communicating with you because I feared to turn upon you the murderous intentions which the criminals in Madrova had in regard to me. I am a doomed man unless there is a revolution in Berania, and my friends would naturally share my fate unless I divorced myself completely from them.

I learn also that a person resembling me is appearing in New York and being treated royally by silly people. I do not expect him to live long.

In regard to myself, have no concern. I am in sanctuary and also earning my living. I do not give you my address lest our correspondence lead to my discovery, but I give you assurances of my most distinguished consideration and trust that the day will come when I can properly show my gratitude to my best friend.

There was no signature, a useless precaution since Carlos identified himself in the letter, but his statement regarding the possibility of the correspondence being traced caused Jervis to frown. He picked up the envelope which he had tossed on his night table, inspected it, and uttered a low ejaculation. The envelope had been steamed open and resealed, and the job had not been a neat one. There was the print of a dirty finger at one corner.

Grandez was in the hospital and likely to remain there for weeks, after which he would be tried and probably sent to prison for burglary and attempted murder. His two gunmen were dead. Nevertheless, a watch was being kept upon Will Jervis and his mail was being opened. Unhappily enough, the only communication he had received from Carlos since landing in America had come at this time. Of course the king had been moved to write because his friend had been wounded, but it was an indiscretion.

Equally strange was the verification of the haphazard statement Will had made to Grandez that Carlos was in California. He *was* in California. And, immediately, the agents of Berania who were in New York would head westward. It was most unlikely that Carlos would evade them for any length of time.

"**HOW LONG** before I can travel, nurse?" Will demanded.

"It will be at least another week before you can walk without limping," she replied.

He laughed. "I don't mind a limp. The wound is healed. Will it injure it if I take a transcontinental train?"

"You'll have to ask the doctor, Mr. Jervis."

"I won't ask him. I'll tell him I'm going."

The nurse looked concerned, and later he heard her phoning from the living room to the doctor. However, despite objections, four days later Will Jervis left New York on the Twentieth Century for Chicago and points west.

In his compartment he had plenty of time to consider his step. Why was he butting into an affair which was none of his business and which was very likely to cost him his life? Why was it that, through all the ages, kings have had the faculty of making people lay down their lives for them, though kings, all through history, have been even less grateful and appreciative of favors than republics? Carlos wasn't his king, and he owed him no loyalty. It was purely by chance that he had been upon the royal flying field in Berania when Carlos fled from his palace. Jervis had acquitted himself well and been discharged from service after he had made it possible for the king to arrive unheralded and unknown in America.

Probably it was because the Aronhof was a stranger in a strange land, without a solitary friend, and with enemies closing in upon him, that Jervis felt it incumbent upon him to go to his assistance.

Furthermore, the king was in immediate danger because of

the friendly impulse which had caused him to write to the young American in New York.

And there was another reason, which Will would not acknowledge to himself. He received a big kick out of a battle. Not for a second during the affair in his apartment had he been frightened, and while the contest was on he was having the biggest thrill of his life. It would be fun to stand shoulder to shoulder with the exiled monarch and help beat off his enemies.

He was confident that he would not add to the perils of King Carlos by going out to California, because the royal enemies were already aware that the Aronhof was hiding out in the Golden State. Nor was he proposing to point the way to the hiding place for the miscreants. He would live quietly, bide his time, get the United States Secret Service to work to locate Carlos. And he might as well be crossing the continent in a drawing-room as convalescing in his apartment in New York.

CHAPTER VI

A PRINCE OF HOLLYWOOD

BEFORE HE HAD been working for the Swaseys a week, Carl Decker found that complications were developing. James Swasey—whose first name had been dropped as being too reminiscent of "Shifty Jim" when Mrs. Mason Swasey's education had proceeded to a point where she understood the meaning of the word Junior—had it in for the chauffeur, and Gladys Swasey was falling in love with him.

Carl found both attitudes annoying. He had discovered peace in the precipitous mountains of Beverly. The high bare hills and the weirdly winding cañons recalled to him the mountains of Berania, and the lovely villas of the Italian and Spanish and Beranian type reminded him of pleasant sojourns upon the Riviera.

He loved machinery as Louis the Sixteenth had loved clockwork. In Madrova he had made a practice of donning overalls and puttering round his own fleet of magnificent motors. He was thoroughly familiar also with airplane machinery, though he had been forced to promise the privy council that he would consider what a national calamity his death would be and keep out of the air. He enjoyed driving and there are few places in the world where a system of perfect roads penetrates to all points in a wild country of surpassing beauty as in California.

Accustomed to uniforms all his life, the blue and gold livery of the Swaseys did not irk him, nor was he humiliated by his service as one less sure of his social position might have been.

43

As a king is the servant of his people, there is no training for service comparable to that of royalty. Everybody knows that a good butler has manners even more magnificent than those of a monarch and the new chauffeur at the Swaseys had dignity, poise, and complete savoir-faire.

In contrast to the other servants at the Swaseys', Carl dominated the scene as the Monument dominates Washington. What went on at the big house did not interest him in the slightest degree. The family existed only to provide him with shelter, food and emoluments. His attitude toward them was so strictly impersonal that Gladys was divided between admiration and exasperation. She found it impossible to get him into conversation and she was unable to extract from him the slightest information about his past.

Mrs. Mason Swasey thought he had lovely manners and looked magnificent in her livery, and his patience when left waiting for her while she shopped and made social calls was sublime.

At first, after leaving him sitting in the car for hours at a time, she returned full of apologies, but Carl, apparently, was quite unperturbed and indifferent to delays.

How could she know that very early in life a king must learn never to be bored, for his career is filled with compulsory attendance at every sort of dull function. Often Carl had been compelled to sit on a hard chair in a reviewing stand while a hundred thousand troops, all dressed exactly alike, marched past.

While Carl gave his employers the consideration they deserved and kept them at arm's length, he was on friendly terms with the servants of the Swaseys. Possessing a keen sense of humor, he was entertained by their assumption that he was a member of their caste. And he was interested in the viewpoint of common folks with whom, for the first time in his life, he was in contact.

He discovered food for thought when he learned that, despite high wages and living conditions not surpassed by the middle class in Berania, the servants were, one and all, discontented, envious and ambitious to step into the millionaire class themselves. He found none of the contentment with their lot which was exhibited by the laboring classes of Berania, and he made a comment in his notebook that the American working people are better off and less satisfied than the working class of any other nation in the world. Not an original observation, but he thought it was.

His evenings were entirely free and he had a small car at his disposal which enabled him to run into town and go to a film show. He liked film shows. He was keenly interested in a news reel which showed the inauguration of the temporary president of Berania, General Rafael Torres, a black-hearted traitor.

He purchased books and had plenty of time to read them. He got started on the memoirs of an exiled king. He was a silent if amused listener at the servants' dining table and he was careful to avoid Miss Swasey, who kept dropping in at the garage on all sorts of pretended errands.

Carl rightly concluded that this big, fine and obviously discontented girl was in a mood to make a fool of herself with a chauffeur and he realized from the firm jaw of Mrs. Mason Swasey that he would be sent about his business as soon as she discovered it.

HOWEVER, his trouble really began on the night when he was called upon to substitute for Clancy and drive Junior Swasey in the Rolls.

Junior Swasey was a blond, rather fat young man with mean blue eyes and a loose lower lip. He was arrogant, tactless and a victim of too much money. He was forced to make use of a chauffeur because the State of California, for excellent reasons, had revoked his driving license. He secured the silence of Tom Clancy by heavy tips.

Carl ran the car under the porte-cochère and waited patiently half an hour for the son and heir who finally emerged wearing a blue serge suit and carrying a small handbag the contents of which the king did not, at the moment, suspect.

Junior hopped into the front seat beside the driver.

"Hollywood," he said. "Sunset Boulevard and Gower."

"Yes, sir."

"How long you been a chauffeur?" asked Swasey.

"Many years, sir."

"Mother hired you without references, didn't she?"

"Yes, sir."

"You told her you had been driving in Europe."

"Yes, sir."

"Well, I think that's a lot of hooey. You want to watch your step, my man."

"I shall, sir."

"You may have to drive me a lot. How are you at minding your own business?"

The king bit his lip. "Excellent," he said curtly.

"My mother is old-fashioned and the less she knows about me the better. Here, take this."

He handed Carl a ten-dollar bill which the monarch accepted as a matter of course because he knew it went with the job.

"Ever hear of the Sphinx?"

Carl smiled. He had been the guest of the King of Egypt at a royal picnic at Gizeh. The King of Abyssinia and the Crown Prince of Italy had been present.

"Yes, sir," he said.

"Well, the better the imitation you give of the Sphinx, the more tips you'll get."

Carl was silent.

The big car sped along Sunset Boulevard and turned south at Gower.

A second later Junior said, "Stop in front of that little white house over there."

The millionaire descended and Carl waited patiently for ten minutes. He was having an unpleasant experience for the first time on the new job. Armored as he was in his own dignity it was impossible for a bounder of this type to insult him, but he hoped that Clancy would recover from his illness immediately so that he would not have to drive Junior again.

At the end of ten minutes Junior came out of the little house accompanied by a young woman. The car had drawn up under a street lamp, the rays of which fell upon the girl as she approached.

Carl gazed upon her and his eyes sparkled with interest and, for no reason, he felt a curious contraction in the region of his heart.

This was the loveliest little creature he had ever seen. She could not have been more than five feet and an inch in her high-heeled slippers. Her figure was exquisitely rounded yet she was not plump. Her legs were slim and her feet were tiny. Her face was small and made to appear smaller by the grandeur of her blue eyes. Her features were exquisite.

She smiled at something said by Junior and there was so much of wistfulness, sweetness and witchery in that smile that the graven image that was Carl Decker was galvanized. He sprang out, threw open the door, and the adorable creature vanished into the interior of the big town car, followed by her escort.

"Drive out through Cahuenga Pass," Junior instructed.

FIVE MINUTES later they were speeding out the boulevard which is the main road to San Francisco, Carl was marveling at the impression this little person had made upon a man before whom all the beauties of Europe had passed in review, and was regretting that a girl so sweet and appealing should be lacking in principle, for to his Continental mind, a young unmarried woman who went driving unchaperoned at night with a man was not reputable.

The flirtations of the son of his employer were none of his

business. In Berania the rich young men preyed upon the pretty girls of the lower classes and he assumed the same thing .went on in America. Lamentable, but nothing to be done about it. This young woman came out of a small, cheap home and, no doubt, expected to profit by her excursion with young Swasey.

Carl tried not to listen to the conversation of his passengers. Until tonight he had not been in the least interested. He caught snatches of Junior's remarks, but the girl spoke in such a low tone he could not hear her. Swasey was narrating at length his exploits upon the polo field and Carl smiled contemptuously to think that a man so much overweight would presume to play a game in which horsemanship and courage are needed as much as the agility which comes from being in training.

He was directed to stop at a road house constructed to resemble a Spanish farmhouse and Junior and the girl descended there. Carl was left outside for nearly three hours while the pair dined and danced. Having had an early dinner himself, he remained in his seat in meditation.

It occurred to him, not for the first time, that he was a very lonely man and doomed to remain so. In Berania, women had thrown themselves at his head to a point where he had no taste for them. He had not married because the brides offered him were impossible to a man with ideals.

In America, he had not failed to observe women and it seemed to him that they had a piquancy which European women lacked. They were more frank, more honest, less sex-conscious and even more beautiful than those across the Atlantic. He thought a man like himself could be happy with the right kind of American girl. Only, he was an exile and a fugitive—at present a servant. He had no taste for amours with housemaids and even in this democratic country cultured young women did not promenade with chauffeurs in livery.

If he did meet and love and marry an American girl, there was always the prospect that Berania would recall him to the throne, and that stiff-necked nation would not stand for a queen who had not been a princess. No, he was fated to remain alone until he regained his kingdom and then he would have to marry one of the eligibles. If there were only a princess as charming as the little creature in the road house with Junior Swasey!

After a long time he fell asleep and was rudely awakened by Swasey.

"Come on there, Decker," said the scion of wealth. "We're on our way."

The girl was already in the car and Junior hopped in. Carl started the motor and turned its nose toward Hollywood. He had proceeded about a mile when Junior leaned forward and tapped him on the shoulder.

"Go up the next turnout on the right," he ordered.

"No, no, please. I want to go right home," said the girl anxiously.

"Do what I tell you," commanded Junior, and immediately pulled up the window which cut off the interior from the driving seat.

CHAPTER VII

THE IMPERFECT CHAUFFEUR

THE PERFECT CHAUFFEUR turned right at the next corner and found himself on a narrow dirt road which ran through a dark and uninhabited cañon.

A moment later the window was pulled down.

"Stop the car," said Junior, and pulled up the window.

Carl was sinking his teeth into his lower lip and his eyes were snapping angrily. Through the glass behind him he heard excited voices within. It appeared that the young woman was not as complaisant as Swasey had anticipated. The King of Berania clenched his hands tightly. He liked that girl.

And then she screamed; not a stage scream, but an anguished appeal for help.

"Ah," said Carl with tremendous relief, "it appears that she is not a courtesan."

He slid out of his seat, tore open the door of the tonneau and stuck in his head.

"I beg your pardon, miss," he said suavely, "is there anything I can do?"

"Yes, yes, please make him let me out of here."

"Damn you!" shouted Junior. "What are you butting in for? Shut that door and go for a walk."

"Would you be just as well satisfied, miss, if the gentleman left the car?" asked Carl mildly.

"I don't care!" exclaimed the young woman. "I want to get away from him. I thought he was a gentleman, but he isn't."

"Kindly step out, Mr. Swasey," requested the chauffeur.

Junior's answer was a bellow of rage. Releasing the girl, he plunged forward and drove his right fist at Carl's head. Carl's left hand grasped the wrist and dragged Junior forward. His right grasped his collar. Deftly and easily he lifted the hundred and seventy pound man out of the machine and tossed him into the ditch five feet distant.

Junior fell prone, scrambled to his feet exploding with profanity and drew a revolver from his pocket which he pointed shakily at the chauffeur.

Carl moved slowly toward him.

"Is it your intention to murder me, Mr. Swasey?" he inquired evenly.

"Yes, you dog. I'll fill you so full of lead they'll never be able to dig it out."

"Indeed," replied Carl, moving a couple of steps nearer. "I understand one may not even shoot a servant in America."

As he spoke his right arm whipped up like the spring of a rattlesnake and his strong hand wrenched the weapon from the fingers of the millionaire.

"Now, Mr. Swasey," he said politely, "I think a walk will do you good. Kindly start in that direction." His gesture was toward the continuation of the cañon road.

"I'll be damned if I do—by Heaven, you'll smart for this."

For Carl had covered him with his own gun and he was already following the direction of the chauffeur's finger.

The chauffeur returned to the car.

"Now, miss," he said, "if you wish, I'll take you home."

"I'll be much obliged," she said quietly.

He closed the door, sprang to his seat, backed the car a hundred feet to a turn-off, maneuvered it into the right direction and stepped on the gas. He was humming a quaint old Beranian folk song as he drove. Careless of the consequences, he was happy because the girl in the back seat was not the sort he had assumed her to be.

AS HE swung into the main road, the window behind him opened.

"Would you mind," she asked plaintively, "if I sat on the front seat with you?"

For answer he drew *up to* the roadside and opened the door for her. The hand she gave him was small and white and soft.

She sank into the seat beside him with a sigh of relief.

"Gracious," she said, "I'm well out of that mess."

"So it would appear," he answered curtly.

"I certainly owe you a ton of gratitude," she declared. Her voice was soft and pleasant and its modulation was charming. It lacked the nasal twang he found in many American voices.

"It was a pleasure to be of service."

"I know exactly what a big thing you did," she continued. "You're going to have trouble over this."

"I am not apprehensive."

"You're English, aren't you?"

"My mother was English."

"You are a remarkable sort of chauffeur," she commented.

"Thank you, miss."

"When you walked up to the gun in that crazy man's hand, you did the bravest thing I ever saw."

"Not at all. He wouldn't have fired."

"Wouldn't he? Mr. Swasey was insanely intoxicated. He drank heavily in the road house and if I could think of any way to get home I would have refused to go with him."

"I rather marveled that a young lady of your sort would have left your home with him," he said significantly.;

She sighed. "I took a chance. One has to take chances in this game."

"What game, please?"

"Why, motion pictures."

"Are you an actress?"

"Trying to be. I met Mr. Swasey at a party a few nights ago.

He is very rich and he told me he would introduce me to a very big producer. So I accepted an invitation to dine with him. Of course I figured that it would probably come to nothing, but it certainly would come to nothing if I turned him down."

"Nevertheless, to accompany a man at night in a motor car unchaperoned—"

She laughed. "Good heavens, you *are* benighted!" she exclaimed. "There are no such things as chaperons in this country, my dear man. Girls know how to take care of themselves."

"Your experience of this evening refutes that."

"Well, I made a mistake but, thanks to you, it wasn't fatal. Most men are very decent. They grow them that way in America, Mr. Europe."

"And of course you will be careful in the future."

"You can count on that," she said, smiling. "Now, you work for Mr. Swasey and you are going to be discharged, aren't you?"

"Very likely."

"And if I hadn't been a fool," she continued, "you would have remained his chauffeur."

"I assure you it is of no moment."

"It's entirely my fault, but I am very glad of it," she said earnestly, "A man like you has no business wearing a livery. I can tell by your speech and your manner and the way you jumped to my rescue that you are a gentleman, a college graduate, too. Aren't you?"

"Perhaps," he said, smiling.

"Well, snap out of it."

"I must earn my living, unfortunately, miss, and driving cars is about the only gainful trade I know."

"Do you realize that you would succeed in motion pictures?" she asked.

"I do not."

"This town is full of beautiful girls, but men of your type are scarce. They'd snap you up. I'll give you a tip; they are looking for a man to play the King of Berania."

THE PERFECT chauffeur was so astonished that the car swerved out of its course.

"Why—why the King of Berania?"

"Oh, they are going to make a big film on that subject. They'll make it some imaginary kingdom, of course, but they'll follow the news as far as his escape from the kingdom. Only, they have it that he loved a lady in Madrova and the republicans imprisoned her so he crossed the frontier, rallied his friends, fought his way to the capital, released the girl and made her his queen and resumed his throne."

"What sublime rubbish," he commented. "No, Miss—er—"

"Dawning—Dalma Dawning. What's your name?"

"Carl Decker, at your service. I have not the slightest intention of becoming an actor. I prefer being a chauffeur."

"But you're going to be fired."

"Then I'll be chauffeur for somebody else."

"That's the trouble with Europeans," she said sadly. "The caste system is ingrained in them. Once a servant, always a servant, though I'm sure you have been something else."

"As there is no caste in America a servant is as good as anybody else."

"To quote you, 'sublime rubbish.' Nobody who wears some one's livery is as good as the person for whom he works."

"Well, my dear young lady, that's a matter of opinion. This, I believe, is your residence."

He brought the car to a stop. She did not move from her seat.

"I'm tremendously grateful," she assured him.

"I consider that I have been privileged."

"Well," she said, hesitating. "Won't I see you again?"

"I'm afraid not. I am a servant, you know."

She tossed her head. "I don't care if you are. I like you. You are a gentleman. I want to see you again."

"Well," he said unsteadily, for her eyes, her smile and her

words had gone to his head, "I shall probably be unemployed to-morrow and not in livery."

"Call for me at eight o'clock. I may work and I can't make a dinner engagement."

"I shall be here."

"Aren't you afraid to go home after what you did to that swine?"

"I am not concerned about him."

She chuckled. "I bet he has to walk miles. Nobody would pick up a man on the road at night and I don't believe there is a place where he could phone for a car within a couple of miles of that side-road."

Carl laughed. "He is overweight. It will do him good."

"Gosh, but you've got a wonderful disposition," she said, laughing. "Well, good night. And I'll be expecting you."

"My failure to appear would be my disappointment."

"I love your stiff English. I was born in Europe myself, but I've been here so long I talk perfect American."

"I thought I did."

She laughed in his face. "You'll learn that you don't if you associate much with me. This is good night."

He saw her go up the path with reluctance and then drove back to Beverly Hills in an exalted mood.

This girl liked him. Many women liked the King of Berania, but Dalma Dawning was not dazzled by rank and glitter. She knew him to be a chauffeur and she despised menials, yet she was willing to be seen in the company of a man who wore livery because she recognized the man beneath. It was the first time that a woman had ever evinced a friendship for the person, not the personage, and this one was the loveliest little creature upon which his eyes had ever rested.

He wasted no thought upon the rage of Junior Swasey and accepted the certainty of his dismissal without concern. It was worth losing the job to have won the esteem of the blond little picture actress.

THE GIRL ON THE TRAIN

WILL JERVIS NOTICED the beautiful brunette upon the observation platform of the Chief as he limped past on his way to his car. His sharp blue eyes usually missed nothing and in the fraction of a second which it took him to pass he noted that she had amazing black eyes, an oval face of perfect line, a very slightly aquiline nose, a ripe red mouth and a determined little chin.

She held her hat on her lap which enabled him to see that her hair was parted in the middle and was of unusual thickness, blackness and luster. It was a Latin face, Italian, Spanish, Roumanian or Beranian. Or she might be Mexican or South American.

Anyway, she was a patrician. She was wearing a smart traveling suit of black and red, and Will did not fail to observe that the foot which she had pushed through the railing of the platform was very small, aristocratic and clad in a French slipper.

She was so vivid and brilliant that she might be one of the foreign film stars of Hollywood, but Will didn't think so because a keen intelligence was carved on her lovely countenance. She intrigued him.

It had been his intention to remain in his quarters until the train arrived at Los Angeles, but the vision on the observation platform made him reconsider. Will Jervis, like King Carlos, had encountered many beautiful women in his career, but, not being a king, he had never been pursued by them. He had been in love, or thought so at the time, upon two or three occasions. Being blond, broad-shouldered and emphatically Nordic in appearance, he was particularly attracted to dark women, but he had never seen one who compared to the girt on the train.

Furthermore, there was something vaguely familiar about her. He didn't think he could ever forget a face like hers, but he couldn't place her and wasn't certain that he had ever encountered her. It must be his familiarity with the type she represented in Madrova, renowned for the loveliness of its brunettes.

He was too tired to leave his drawing-room that night, but he awakened at eight thirty next morning and decided to make the journey to the dining car on the chance that she might be having breakfast there. It was a remote chance. A girl of her type would probably have a compartment and breakfast in bed, or, if she were in a section, she would sleep as late as possible.

The dining car was two cars ahead. Will's wound hurt him slightly when he walked and he had a pronounced limp, but he thought he could manage the trip by moving slowly and leaning on the backs of seats. He was entering the second car and had passed the compartments when he saw the toes of a pair of tiny French slippers protruding from beneath the curtains of a berth.

He moved carefully forward, his eyes glued to the shoes, and he was almost upon them when the curtains of the berth unexpectedly opened and a young woman, the wearer of the shoes, collided with him.

THE SHOCK was slight, but it was sufficient, combined with the surprise and the rocking of the train, to cause him to lose his balance, tip backward, grasp at the opposite seat for support and fall heavily into it. A twinge from his wound caused him to groan.

An expression of deep concern was registered upon the lovely face.

"*Mon Dieu, monsieur!*" she exclaimed. "A thousand pardons. 'Ave I 'urt you?"

He smiled up at her. "It was my fault and no harm done."

She leaned over him. Her lips were like cherries and her teeth whiter than fresh fallen snow. "But you groan! You are 'urt!"

"I am recovering from an injury to my leg. It's a little weak."

"But you should not try to walk. You are not wise, *monsieur*."

He grinned. "I started for the dining car, and I'm going to make it."

"But I, also, go to the dining car. I will 'elp you, *monsieur*."

Will endeavored to conceal his satisfaction. "Please don't trouble about me. I can ring for the porter if I need help."

"I am strong," she insisted. "You will place a hand on my shoulder. Come, try."

As he could think of nothing more delightful than to place a hand upon such a beautiful shoulder, he protested no more, but rose, touched her lightly and moved down the aisle with her. This charming little affair had taken place with no apparent witnesses, though several berths had not been put up and there might be interested listeners behind the curtains.

"You should not be traveling alone in your condition," she protested.

He laughed. "I assure you I am practically well. In another two or three days the leg won't bother me at all."

They arrived at the dining car, and the steward, assuming that they were together, indicated a table for two. She hesitated.

"Since you have been so kind," he said eagerly, "may I presume further and ask you to breakfast with me?"

"Well, why not?" she challenged, and seated herself without further ado.

Will slipped into the chair opposite her and considered that he had already been repaid for his journey. She was dainty, chic as a Parisienne, radiant as a Spaniard; of her kindliness he had already had a sample.

She ordered rolls, butter and coffee. As Will had already been converted to the Continental breakfast, he did likewise.

"May I introduce myself? My name is Jervis," he said.

"Merci, monsieur. I am Aimee LeFevre."

"Then you are French? I did not think so."

"I am originally from Provence!" she exclaimed.

"Then you are far from home."

"And I am going farther—to Los Angeles."

"Motion pictures?"

"In a way. I am a novelist. My work has been translated into English and will be made into a film."

"Congratulations. What is the name of your work?"

" 'Le Maison Bleu.' "

"But that was written by Reine de la Reine."

"How you are *instruite!*" she exclaimed. "That is a pen name."

Will's face was almost without expression, but there was a sinking feeling in the pit of his stomach. This was a lie. He knew Reine de la Reine. She was a French woman of middle age with an incipient mustache who had spent a winter in Madrova and dined at the house of the American ambassador.

WILL JERVIS, shrewd man of the world, had been upon the point of falling, like a boy, in love with the exquisite prevaricator. He was instantly on his guard.

"And you are traveling alone, an unmarried Frenchwoman? I observe you wear no ring."

She laughed merrily. "But I am emancipated, my friend. You 'ave no idea 'ow we 'ave broken down conventions in Paris. I am a graduate of the Sorbonne. I am unmarried, but not a poor little *jeune fille.*"

"And are you enjoying yourself?"

"I 'ave been bored on these trains. The journeys are so long."

"When did you land?"

"A week ago in New York. *Monsieur,* is your first name Vill?"

Will, who spoke French almost as well as he spoke English, was not deceived by her accent. It was very much like that of a cultured French person speaking English fluently, but not quite.

"Yes," he said curtly.

"Then it is you who have flown away from Madrova with the King of Berania and who 'ave been shot by burglars in New York not long ago. That is why you are lame."

"I see that you read the papers," he said dryly.

Mlle. LeFevre clapped her hands joyfully. "But this is an 'onor, *monsieur*. You are a gr-reat man."

"I can't agree to that."

"That poor king," she said. "I 'ave been so sorry for 'im because he was so 'andsome. And he was a good king, too. Do you know, I 'ave seen 'im in New York?"

"I read that somebody whom the papers insist is Carlos has been seen around town, but I understand he denies it."

"Oh, but it is he. I know him. I have seen him in Madrova, where I spent the winter."

Another lie.

"Did you speak to him in New York?" Will asked casually.

"Mon Dieu, no, but I 'ave seen him at a theater."

"Well, he's a nice chap, and I hope he likes America."

"Then you 'ave not seen him, and you are his friend?"

"You forget I was wounded by burglars and have seen no one."

"Yet it was in the papers. Surely he has written you?"

"Kings have short memories, *mademoiselle*."

"Vraiment. You will come and talk to me some time during this dreadful journey? One gets tired of reading."

"With pleasure," he said truthfully. It was a pleasure to sit near her and watch the play of expressions upon her clever and mendacious little face. What was her game, he wondered?

Jervis returned to his drawing-room. He need not have worried, he thought bitterly, about his chances of making her acquaintance. She was upon the train for that purpose. She was no more a French girl than she was the popular novelist, Reine de la Reine. The young woman was a Beranian. She had seemed vaguely familiar. Well, she was a member of some cultured family of Madrova whom he had seen at a dance or reception while he was in the embassy. Republicanism had been a cult among the intelligentsia of Berania. It was natural for rich and educated families who could not possibly break into the ranks of the nobility to desire a state of affairs where titles would be abolished. This girl was an agent of the so-called republic.

Her purpose was to vamp him and, through him, discover the whereabouts of King Carlos. He hoped she was not aware that her principals wished to do more than keep the menace to the republic under close observation.

It was a great pity, for, if she were what he had hoped at first, he would have fallen in love with the girl. She had everything he demanded in a woman, but—she wasn't honest.

Like Grandez, she had led the conversation deftly round to the puppet in New York. Was it possible that Grandez had not yet had a chance to communicate with his confederates and they were not yet certain whether Jervis had penetrated the mask of the impostor?

CHAPTER IX

TRICKED!

AS THE TRAIN sped westward toward Los Angeles, Will Jervis tried to fathom the mysterious conduct of his and Carlos's foes.

What was the object of the exhibition of the double of the ex-king in New York? There was no question in Will's mind that he was an agent of Berania. Was it their intention to have the masquerader go in for riotous living and blatant immorality, to spend money wildly and thus substantiate the charge that Carlos had sequestered millions of the money of the Beranian people?

Did they hope to disgust the royalists by creating the impression that the king was a drunkard and a libertine? If they did they were fools, for the bad moral character of a king has never much perturbed his subjects. In fact, the common people rather admire a ruler who is a "hell of a good fellow."

Anyway, Mlle. LeFevre was out to bewitch the king's American friend, Will Jervis, and he had to admit that, if they had consulted him personally regarding the sort of a woman who would be best calculated to make a fool of him, they could not have chosen better.

It would be interesting to watch her performance. He would give her all the rope she needed. Forewarned, she would not wheedle anything out of him, but he would use her to relieve the tedium of the journey.

Was he in any danger during the journey? There was no

telling. And once he had arrived—well, Los Angeles County is as big as several Eastern States and is populated by a couple of million people. Unless Carlos were exhibiting himself out there as his double was doing in New York they would not locate him readily; but their enemies would assume that Jervis might lead them to him. Let *mademoiselle* exercise all her wiles. He was on his guard.

Endeavoring to dismiss the delectable spy from his mind, he picked up one of a number of magazines which he had stocked, but found it very difficult to concentrate. The train was crossing the historic but exceedingly monotonous plains of Kansas. There was no harm in talking to the girl since he knew all about her.

That there was about Latin women of her type a stimulating vivacity and an exotic fascination which American girls seldom possess, he had always been convinced. It had been delightful to watch the play of expressions upon her piquant features and it would be fun to match wits with the little rogue.

He worked his way to her car, but found her section empty and, with no little physical distress, he continued on to the club car where his search was rewarded.

Mlle. LeFevre was there, but, to his annoyance, she was talking to a big, broad-shouldered, swarthy, black-eyed man whom he thought at first sight to be one of her fellow conspirators, but upon closer view decided to be an American Hebrew with a long instead of an aquiline nose and a much too ponderous chin.

The girl spied him upon his entrance, smiled and beckoned to him.

"Mr. Jervis," she said, "I want to present you to Mr. Goldsmith who makes the motion pictures."

Goldsmith rose, and, observing that Will was lame, aided him to a place in the leather-covered section where he and the young woman had been sitting.

"What a coincidence, *monsieur!*" she exclaimed. "I find on

The assassin whirled and fell on his face.

the train the gentleman who 'ave engage me to supervise the
filming of my novel."

"President of Mammoth Pictures, Inc.," said Goldsmith
complacently. "Say, Miss LeFevre has been telling me that you
are the feller who rescued the King of Berania."

"I flew him to Paris, yes," replied Will, a trifle annoyed.

"What a break! I tell you, in conscience, though it 'll be in
all the papers soon, that I just pulled off the biggest coup in the
history of the business."

"It's truly marvelous," declared the girl.

"Just before leaving New York I signed a contract with the
King of Berania for a picture," declared Goldsmith trium-
phantly.

"Good Lord! You mean you have signed up the fellow whom
the papers claim to be the king."

"He is the king. You understand, though, that he is in—what
you call it—"

"Incognito."

"Yep. We can't bill him as King Carlos, but we don't have to. By the time we get through, everybody in America will know who he is even if we put him out in the 'Fall of a Throne' as Alfonso Gomez with quotation marks round the name."

"That seems to have been quite an achievement," said Will politely.

"Do you suppose his majesty can act?" asked the girl.

"I have a notion that he is a fine actor," said Will significantly. He watched her eyes as he spoke, but they revealed nothing.

"We'd make an actor out of him if he was a horse or a dog," said the producer. "Now, Mr. Jervis, I just got another big idea. You got kicked out of the government service for carrying off this king. You need the money. I can use you in the fillum."

The proposition was so unexpected and so utterly preposterous that Will guffawed.

GOLDSMITH scowled. "It ain't a laughing matter. If this king don't think he's too good for pictures where do you get off giving them the razz?"

"I beg your pardon, I was laughing at the notion of turning actor myself."

"Why not?" demanded the girl vivaciously. "You would make much money and be very much entertained, *monsieur.*"

"And you and the king are old pals," urged Goldsmith. "And having you along with him clinches it. Say, it's the biggest thing in the history of the game."

"How about the prime minister and the first lord of the treasury. Can't you sign them up?"

"I cabled Madrova," replied Goldsmith, who saw nothing absurd in the suggestion, "but those birds are in jail and the republic won't let 'em out, even if I give bond to return them when I'm through with 'em."

Will met Aimee LeFevre's eyes and saw that she was as much amused as himself.

"Count me out," he said crisply. "Set it down to stage fright. I am not going into motion pictures. It's my last word."

"I'll get the king to call on you when he comes out here. He'll line you up," said Goldsmith, undaunted. "You're like a lot of people that don't know this game is bigger than anything in the world. We could buy and sell a lot of them ten-cent king-doms, though Berania is the biggest country that we have tackled yet."

"If you want your picture to have a happy ending and yet stick to facts," suggested Will, "why not turn out the Beranian government and set the king on his throne again—of course, after you have finished with him?"

"Which ain't a bad idea. I'd do it if it could be done cheap enough."

"Monsieur is a remarkable man," declared Mlle. LeFevre. "He 'ave insist that I arrive in Hollywood with a different name."

"I hired Reine de la Reine," declared the producer. "Nobody ever heard of Miss LeFevre and nobody can pronounce that name, so she gets off the train with the moniker that's on her book. This young lady is a lot more reasonable than you are, Mr. Jervis."

"TELEGRAM for Mr. Goldsmith," called a porter. The pro-ducer called him, opened his message and scowled.

"Every time I turn my back," he complained, "them fellows in Hollywood go haywire. I got to go to my drawing room and write a lot of letters."

The young woman made a moue at his retreating back, met Will's eyes and they both smiled.

"He is a true species of camel," she exclaimed.

"Enterprising, though," Will observed. "I wonder how much he is paying this Alfonso person."

"No matter what he pays, he will make a fortune from the

picture. It is the first time a true king has agreed to appear in the screen."

"Carlos must have changed a lot," Will reflected. "He struck me as a man of much pride and magnificent dignity."

"It cannot be the money," she said, "He has tremendous investments in America and England."

"That is not true. He told me himself that he had nothing. The tale was put out by the republicans to prevent him from awakening the sympathy of his loyal subjects."

She looked interested. "I did not know that. I read that he 'ad escaped with the crown jewels which are immensely valuable."

"I assure you they were not in my aëroplane. If they were it would not have been able to leave the ground. The crown jewels of Berania weigh tons."

"Ah, but he could have taken a few of the most valuable of the diamonds and rubies."

"He had no luggage."

Covertly Will studied her. Was it possible that he had jumped to a conclusion? While he knew she was not Reine de la Reine, Goldsmith confirmed her statement that she was going to Hollywood to supervise the making of one of Reine de la Reine's novels into a film and Goldsmith was blatantly a producer and nothing else.

Jervis didn't want to think Mlle. LeFevre a spy of the Beranian government, but she was certainly an impostor of some sort. If he had not been a diplomat he would probably have quizzed her about Reine de la Reine and forced her to admit deception, but he preferred to study her further and give her no inkling of his suspicions. He did not even shift the conversation to the French language in which he knew he could detect a Beranian accent if one were present.

To tell the truth, he was content to bask in her smiles and listen to the ripple of her pleasant voice with its very creditable struggle with the English tongue.

She was the first to depart from the car, and he remained an hour alone in the chair car before he undertook the laborious trip back to his drawing room.

When he entered it, he uttered an ejaculation of dismay and anger, for his big pigskin traveling bag lay open upon the sofa and upon the chair rested his neat pigskin hand-bag which was equipped with a special lock and which had been ruthlessly sliced open with a knife.

CHAPTER X

THE SECRET SERVICE MAN

HE MADE A quick examination. Everything had been ransacked. A wallet containing money and important letters had not been taken, but the decoration of the Lion of Berania, which he had placed in the small bag for safe keeping, had disappeared.

He reached for the bell button, then his hand dropped to his side.

Useless to give the alarm. An hour ago the train had stopped at Emporia. He remembered that the alleged novelist had left him just after the train pulled out of the station.

Goldsmith had left them three-quarters of an hour earlier. So the man was not a motion picture producer. He was a Jew but a Beranian Jew. While the girl held him in conversation, Goldsmith had entered his drawing room and ransacked his luggage. He had stolen the highly prized decoration. Why?

All Will's suspicions regarding Mlle. LeFevre returned tenfold. The pair had made a complete fool of him. It did not occur to him to doubt their twaddle about the motion picture business. With a sense of humor which Will had to admire, Goldsmith had offered him a job as an actor.

Well, their search had benefited them only in respect to the decoration. There were but forty of these in the world, and the little gold lions were marvelous specimens of the goldsmith's craft.

There was no possibility that any of the members of the order would relinquish his decoration and no goldsmith in the world was clever enough to copy it. The loss was irreparable. Suddenly Will realized—it was most unlikely that the faker in New York possessed one though he sported the silken rosette which was its symbol. The faker's need of the decoration might explain the search.

Goldsmith would have got off at the last station; necessity of sending long telegrams his excuse. Well, he would have him apprehended.

A knock sounded upon the drawing room door. Will opened it and found himself facing an unknown man.

"Yates is the name," he said in a low tone. "United States secret service."

"You are as welcome as the flowers in May," declared Jervis. "Come right in."

He closed the door after his visitor had entered and inspected the person who was reputed to be the cleverest detective working for Uncle Sam. If Yates had been on the train from Chicago Will had not noticed him, but he was not a type to draw attention.

He was a thin, wiry man of about thirty-six or eight. He had a narrow face, nondescript features, wore a small straw-colored mustache and rimless glasses.

His hair was thin and sandy. He wore a light brown suit, in need of pressing. His manner was meek. Behind the glasses were a pair of deceptively timid blue eyes.

"Your credentials?" asked Jervis. This was the last person in the world he would have judged to be a great criminal investigator.

Yates drew a letter from his breast pocket and handed it over with a quiet little smile.

"They always ask for my credentials," he said dolefully.

It was a note from Assistant Secretary of State Downes.

Introducing William Yates, of whom I spoke to you recently. You can rely on him.

"Shake," invited Will. "I've just had a visitor."

"I see. Lose much?"

"The decoration of the Lion of Berania presented to me by King Carlos of Berania. That appears to be all. Where did you come from?"

"Boarded the train at Kansas City last night. Saw you talking to a young lady at breakfast and was sitting in the club car when you were with her and Goldsmith."

"You know him? He's an agent of Berania."

"News to me," said Yates, smiling slightly. "He's a bigwig in the film game in Hollywood."

Will sank into his seat, bewildered. Another theory shattered.

"**MAYBE** you know the girl," he muttered.

"Stranger to me."

"Then who the devil went through my bags and destroyed this one?"

"Don't know. Did you lock your door when you went out?"

"I didn't think of it. How do you happen to be going to California?"

"Same reason you are. To pick up the king."

"Then you know he is in California?"

"Found that out."

"How, may I ask?"

Yates chuckled softly. "This is a new job to us," he said, "this wet-nursing an exiled king. The man we put on it located him in New York and didn't worry much about him. Carlos checked out of the hotel, went directly to the Grand Central Terminal, bought a ticket and signed a fake name to it—Charles Parker."

"Then how did you check him?"

"It took time. I copied his signature at the hotel registry, studied signatures upon ticket stubs sold by all the railroads that day, and finally found 'Charles Parker.' He didn't disguise his hand. When I found he had gone to Los Angeles, you had already started West. I took an airplane to Kansas City and boarded your train. It was a simple job. My predecessor did the same thing, but missed this particular signature."

"Well, he's somewhere in Los Angeles, but I don't know where."

"I'll dig him out. Suppose you tell me, Mr. Jervis, what's on the inside of this. Berania has a republic, Carlos is out, and that's that. Mr. Downes insists he is in great danger. Why?"

As briefly as possible Will explained, and Yates listened with a vacant expression.

"We've had a few Presidents assassinated ourselves," he commented, "and we hold the world's record for cold-blooded murders. If this is a fake republic, run by a gang of crooks, it's a cinch they won't rest until they put the ex-king on ice. The worst place he could have gone is Los Angeles."

"Why?"

"We have a stiff immigration examination at New York, but the Mexican border is easy to cross, and Mexicans come in freely. As these Latin peoples all look alike to our eyes, there is nothing to stop Beranians from coming over the border, doing the job, and getting back in Mexico before the body is discovered."

"I hadn't thought of that phase of it."

"Think this girl is one of them?"

"I did, but I don't know what to think now."

"She may be, but it's a cinch Goldsmith isn't hooked up with her. She could be pinch hitting for this lady novelist and working out her contract in Los Angeles, and at the same time be an information bureau for Berania. Vampish looking dame."

"I think she is amazingly beautiful," declared Will resentfully.

"Sure. The more beautiful they are, the better their stuff works. I'll keep an eye on her."

"Don't you think we need more than one man in Los Angeles if conditions are as you say?"

Yates shrugged. "Point is that, officially, it isn't known that Carlos is in the United States. We've only a small force, and if half a dozen men were planted around him, somebody would rise up in Congress to ask what for. And if the Executive Department explained that we were guarding an exiled king, all the Democrats and Progressives and most of the Republicans would pass a law to chuck out any exiled king that sneaked into this country in disguise."

"But the State Department connived at his arrival here."

"Maybe so, but the State Department isn't going to admit any such thing to Congress. The President is going to be astonished at this breach of the immigration laws and ask Carlos to leave immediately."

"That is exactly what would happen," admitted Jervis.

Yates nodded. "I'm supposed to be out here looking for some Federal mail violators. Technically, that's what we are supposed to be doing when we are guarding the President of the United States. There is no provision in law for a Presidential bodyguard."

"All right. Who broke into my luggage?"

"Give me a few minutes, please."

WILL lit a cigarette as Yates inspected the bags closely. He gave particular attention to the small hand bag. Five minutes passed.

"I can tell you this much," he said. "It was a woman. She cut the bag with a small penknife which she took out of a hand bag containing manicure things and toilet articles. She wore a pair of cloth gloves, suede color. She uses a perfume called 'Cœur d'Eros,' brunette powder, number three shoe—"

"Jumping Jehoshaphat!" exclaimed Jervis. "What color were her eyes, and what is her favorite play."

Yates chuckled in his curious way. "This was a cinch," he said. "She stuck her hand into her bag and, having gloves on, fumbled around. Powder is always leaking out of those little boxes they carry, and she got some on her gloves. In taking it out, she spilled a little on the carpet. Any one could see that."

"I did, but I thought it was talc out of my bag."

"It's darker and finer, She stepped in it and left a faint imprint on the carpet. See. A number three shoe. Women spill perfume all over themselves and it gets on their gloves. I've studied perfumes. This Heart of Cupid—that's the English name—is very rare and expensive stuff, and you can't mistake it. She grabbed the handle of your bag tightly when she was cutting it, and I got a whiff. A thread tore off her glove. See, there it is. Suede color. So I know she's a brunette, probably about five feet one or two, with a peculiar perfume."

"You don't look it," said Will admiringly, "but you are a very remarkable man."

"Looking dumb is one of my best assets."

"Do you know," Jervis said reluctantly, "that you have described Mlle. LeFevre?"

"Frenchwomen go in for cloth gloves in summer more than American women. Does she use this perfume?"

Will smelled of the bag handle. "I don't notice any odor."

"Well, I've a cultivated sense of smell. She's a brunette, about five feet three; but she didn't do it."

"I hope you are certain."

"Positive. She was in the club car when you arrived, and after she left you she did not come near your drawing room."

"How do you know?"

"Because I have a seat two sections away from here, and I followed her when she left you."

"Ah, you suspected her then."

Yates gave a hearty chuckle. "No, I liked her. I mean I liked to look at her."

"This places the robbery as having happened before she left me, if you have been in this car since."

"Right."

"Is there another woman answering that description on the train?"

"Two cars back is a dame about her size and wearing a number three shoe. I wasn't near enough to notice her perfume. She's as homely as a hedge fence."

"Make some excuse to get close to her."

"She would have left the train at Emporia. I'll telegraph back. You see, it was a cinch you'd discover the robbery as soon as you came back from the club car so the thief naturally got off."

"Hurry and make sure, and look for other suspects."

"That one and your friend are the only two who answer the description."

"You don't know who are in the compartments and drawing rooms?"

"Don't I?" replied Yates, grinning. "At nine this morning, wearing a conductor's uniform, I looked over every person on this train."

Will gaped at him.

"But why? You didn't know of this situation then."

THE DETECTIVE'S eyes twinkled. "You'd be surprised how many people Uncle Sam is looking for. Whenever I board a train, I make a complete inspection of the passengers. I picked up a murderer we had been hunting for three years, in connection with a post office robbery, in a Twentieth Century compartment, only two months ago."

"Will you give me your candid opinion? Is Mlle. LeFevre all right?" Will asked eagerly.

Yates hesitated. "I'll tell you. If she was an American I could take one look at her and tell you if she was a crook or on the level, but I don't know much about foreign dames. All I know is that this one is a sure winner in a beauty contest for Miss Universe."

"Let's shake on that," proposed Jervis enthusiastically. "Say, we're slowing down."

"Coming into Newton, Kansas. I'll wire back to find out what became of that homely woman who got off at the last stop."

He left the room. Will, delighted that as clever a man as Yates had so completely exonerated the lovely European girl, watched the train pull into a small station. Beside the station platform was the highway, and several cars were drawn up in anticipation of the arrival of the express.

He saw Yates run along the platform toward the station building, a yellow telegraph form in his hand. A moment or two later a hand tapped upon the window of his drawing room. Supposing it was Yates standing below who wished to communicate with him, Will rose to lift the window, looked down, and saw a shabbily dressed man wearing a golf cap. He caught a glimpse of a pair of small, staring black eyes, and then an automatic in the fellow's right hand. He threw himself back upon his seat as the window pane was shattered by a bullet followed instantly by two others. They whined past him and tinkled against the steel wall of the compartment, flattened, and dropped to the floor.

Unhurt, Will looked out without standing up and saw his would-be murderer running across the platform toward a car twenty feet distant. There was a man in the machine who threw open the door.

"Catch him! Stop him!" shouted Jervis through the shattered window.

Crack, crack, crack! The staccato of an automatic. The gunman who had almost reached the automobile threw up both hands, whirled, and fell on his face.

The train had already begun to move slowly forward, but its progress was checked. Yates was visible now, shooting at the automobile which had swung out of line and was tearing down the highway. It kept on going, apparently unhit.

Yates bent over the body of the assassin and straightened up

as he was descended upon by the stationmaster, the train conductor and a policeman who seemed to spring from the ground.

He satisfied them quickly and led them to the broken
window.

"Were you hit, Mr. Jervis?" he asked anxiously.

"No. Missed by three bullets."

CHAPTER XI

A LADY WHO WAS TOO KIND

WHEN THE MAN who called himself Carl Decker awakened on the morning after his unpleasant encounter with Junior Swasey, he packed his bags before he presented himself at the servants' dining room for breakfast. Afterward he returned to the big garage, busied himself removing the dust of the night before from the Rolls Royce, and waited for the ax to fall. A hour had passed when Junior Swasey came through the garage door.

"You're through," he snarled when he caught sight of the chauffeur.

"Pardon me, sir, but as I was engaged by Mrs. Swasey, I shall have to be discharged by her."

"You'll get out of here immediately on my say so," declared Junior.

"Sorry, sir," said the perfect chauffeur. "I cannot consider it."

"Where's my gun?" Junior demanded surlily.

"I have placed it in the side pocket of your car."

"I've a good mind to use it on you, you rat."

"You have no such desire, Mr. Swasey," said the chauffeur calmly. "You are not drunk at present, and, drunk or sober, you are a coward."

Junior clenched his fist and his eyes shot fire.

"I am not a boxer," said the king. "If you attack me, I'll break a wrench over your head. I am not a coward."

Junior's eyes met his, and he realized that the man meant exactly what he said.

"Furthermore, I do not propose to converse with you," continued Carl. "Inform your mother that you were prevented by me from assaulting an innocent girl; that I threw you out of the car; that you drew a weapon and aimed it at me; that after I had disarmed you I left you in the road, took the young lady home, and returned the car to the garage. Tell her all that, and if she wishes to discharge me I shall be glad to leave."

"I'll tell her it was a put-up job between you and the damned frail," replied Junior furiously. "I'll tell her you're a blackmailer. I'll put detectives on you and dig up a criminal record. I'll land you in jail—that's what I'll do."

"Tell her what you please," said Carl contemptuously.

"If it's the last thing I ever do," shouted Junior, "I'll put you behind the bars."

Carl stooped over, turned a little wheel at the base of the garage wall, picked up the nozzle of the hose, and turned a stream of water full in the face of the son of his employer. He shut it off hastily when a shadow darkened the door and he recognized Miss Swasey.

"By God," screamed Junior, "for that I'll kill you."

"An accident, Junior," said Gladys, smiling significantly. "It might have happened to me."

"What in heck are you doing here?" demanded her half-insane brother.

"I want Decker to take me to the country club."

"He's fired. I just fired him, but first I'm going to beat him within an inch of his life."

Junior, being a trifle larger than the chauffeur and confident in his assurance that Carl was not a boxer, plunged at Decker, swinging like a gate. Carl sidestepped him, grasped his right arm, twisted it, tapped his biceps in a peculiar manner and Junior screamed with agony.

"I did not mention that I am rather skillful at jiu jitsu," Carl said evenly. "Please accept my apology for this scene, Miss Swasey."

He thrust Junior away from him.

"You need not apologize, Decker," the young woman said pleasantly. "Hearing an altercation as I approached, I stopped and listened."

Junior's rage was turned on her.

"You sneaking eavesdropper," he howled. She turned calm blue eyes upon him.

"You are unfit for human companionship," she said contemptuously. "I have heard rumors of your exploits with working girls. I have no doubt that things happened exactly as Decker stated them. You go and tell mother anything you like and I'll tell her the facts."

"Look here, Gladys," her brother said with a swift change of attitude, "you wouldn't be rotten enough to tell her that stuff."

"I would like to spare her feelings, but I am not going to have an honest young man discharged for doing what anybody with an ounce of decency would have done."

"Well," he answered sullenly, "I'll say nothing about it. As for you, Decker, if you're smart you'll make tracks out of here. Things are not going to be pleasant for you from now on."

"If my brother tries to make trouble for you in any way," said Miss Swasey, "I will appreciate it if you will come to me. Junior has tried our patience to a point where it won't last much longer. Mother is not blind, Junior."

"Give me my gun," he said morosely.

Carl removed it from the front door pocket and handed it to him, hilt toward him. His face was without expression.

"Which car do you wish, Miss Swasey?" he asked respectfully.

"The Lincoln runabout."

Junior moved toward the door. "I hope it crashes and you both break your necks," he said piously as he retreated.

CARL seated himself behind the wheel of the roadster and Gladys, who was in golfing clothes, climbed in beside him. In a moment they were moving slowly down the steep winding mountain road.

"I presume he tried to bribe you to be complaisant last night," she said thoughtfully.

"If you don't mind, miss, I would rather not discuss it. I regret that you overheard our conversation."

"I trust that the presence of such a person in our family will not drive you away from us," she said eagerly.

"I should be sorry to go."

"Decker, you are a gentleman, are you not?"

"I am a chauffeur, miss."

"I am certain you have been a soldier."

"In common with all classes of Europeans."

"You are, obviously, a person of refinement. I suspect that your skill with automobiles was gained by driving your own car."

He kept his eyes on the road, The girl was sweet and kind, but she made him almost as uncomfortable as did her brother.

"Junior is a victim of too much money," she said sadly. "He was a decent little boy, but years at school and college with a ridiculously large allowance and my mother's indulgence since his graduation have ruined him. It was cowardly of him to attack you after you had informed him that you were not a boxer."

Carl smiled. He had provocation. "I turned the hose on him purposely."

"I suspected that. Was this a pretty girl, last night?"

"Very pretty."

"Are you sure your interference was really desired by her?"

"Positive," he said, with resentment at her question.

"A picture girl, I presume."

"I believe so."

"They have a bad reputation."

"My dear Miss Swasey," he said angrily, "your brother's intended victim was quite as respectable as you are."

She flushed and was silent. After a minute she said gently.

"If you say so, I do not doubt it. Is there anything I can do
for her?"

"Please accept my apology for my abruptness," he said con-
tritely. "I wish to observe proper respect for my employer."

"I wish you wouldn't be quite so respectful," she replied. "You
are not an ordinary chauffeur but, if you were, my mother took
in washing and my father was a common laborer in the field.
It is an accident that we are wealthy and you are poor."

"Please, Miss Swasey," he pleaded, most uncomfortable, "do
not let us discuss this sort of thing. I am your chauffeur. I am
not resentful of my situation."

"But you won't always be a chauffeur, You are capable of big
things."

The girl of the night before had said almost the same thing
and it had warmed the cockles of the exile's heart. Miss Swasey's
confidence in him alarmed him. She was as ready as her brother
to kick over the traces although in a different way. Fortunately,
their arrival at the Country Club put an end to an embarrassing situation.

"I shall be busy for three or four hours," she said as she
stepped out of the car. "If you like you can go to the beach and
swim instead of waiting here on this sun-burned field."

He touched his cap. "Thank you, miss," he said gratefully.

It was evident to him that the peace he supposed he had
found was not to be lasting. Either the brother or the sister
would force him from his haven in the hills. In the meantime,
the thought of a bath in the ocean appealed to him. The last
time he had gone swimming in the sea was at Biarritz, and the
French police had roped off the beach and kept everybody
except the royal party out of the ocean that morning.

He drove slowly toward Santa Monica, deep in reflections

which were not entirely unhappy. To-night he was going to keep a tryst with a lovely little American girl who liked him despite the fact that he was a chauffeur and wore a livery.

CHAPTER XII

ONE AGAINST THREE

THAT NIGHT CARLOS left his dinner coffee untouched, excused himself and hastened to his quarters. He doffed his livery and put on a plain blue serge suit, picked up a soft white hat and went below to the garage where he chose the small roadster which Mrs. Swasey had informed him he might use when off duty.

Clancy, the other chauffeur, was puttering round the Rolls. He had been in town and had not appeared at dinner.

"Going girling?" he asked cheerfully.

Carl did not answer.

"How did you make out with Junior last night?" demanded Tom. "Get a big tip?"

Carl looked annoyed. He had forgotten completely that he had accepted from the unspeakable Swasey a ten dollar bill at the beginning of the adventure of the previous night, a bribe, of course, to make him deaf, dumb and blind, and a payment which he certainly had not earned.

He thrust his hand into his pocket, drew forth the ten dollars and tossed it at Clancy. "It's yours, take it," he said disgustedly.

"Say, I wasn't trying to make you give up."

"Pick it up or burn it up," Carl said indifferently and drove out of the garage.

Clancy stooped and picked up the ten dollars. He was regarding it affectionately and marveling at the folly of the man who had tossed it away when Junior entered.

"Oh, you're about again," he said unpleasantly. "Where did you get that money?"

"Decker," confessed Clancy. "He said you gave it to him last night and it belonged to me."

Junior snatched it from his hand. "I ought to dock you a week's wages for shamming illness," he snarled. "Get into the car immediately. I'm in a hurry."

With a tolerant shrug, Clancy obeyed orders. Junior jumped in beside him.

"Corey's gambling house and step on it," he commanded.

"But it ain't open until ten o'clock, boss."

"There will be people there I want to see."

Halfway down the hill they sighted Decker in the little roadster.

"Slow up and follow that rat," commanded young Swasey.

They pursued the roadster down Hollywood Boulevard to Gower and, when Carl turned right, Junior mumbled something profane.

"Just as I thought," he said. "Now go to the gambling joint."

CARL rang the bell at the little frame house. He was aware with a sense of surprise that, for the first time in his life when he was going to meet a woman, he was excited.

She opened the door for him. She wore a trim little black suit and black hat from beneath which gold strands peeked coyly out.

She had a cane in her left hand and leaned on it.

"Oh," she said. "You haven't got it on. I was afraid—"

"The livery? I don't wear it off duty. Why are you carrying a cane, Miss Dawning?"

"I turned my ankle at the studio today. It's nothing of any consequence except, if you want to dance, it will have to be some other night."

"I'll be content just to talk," he said eagerly.

"Then that's all right," she said cheerfully. "Where shall we go?"

"Wherever you like."

"I'd rather like to drive down toward the beach. It's a hot night and there will be hundreds of beach parties. Their bonfires along the shore are worth seeing."

He assisted her solicitously into the car and then took the wheel. The cane was placed between them.

"Do you know the road?"

"I had a swim this afternoon at Santa Monica. I went straight out Wilshire Boulevard."

"Go out Sunset to Beverly, It's longer, but a prettier ride and it reaches the beach beyond Santa Monica. Did you lose your job?" she asked anxiously as he threw the car into gear.

HE CHUCKLED. "Not at all. It appears that young Swasey doesn't care to tell his mother why he is vexed with me and I refused to leave at his request."

"But he can tell her lies. She will believe him."

"It happened that Miss Swasey overheard us in argument and said she would inform her mother of the facts. He went off vowing vengeance."

"He is a very rich man, Mr. Decker, and you are a poor one. Oh, I wish I hadn't been fool enough to go out with him, last night."

"I'm delighted. Otherwise we should not have met."

"But I've got you into serious trouble."

"My dear young lady, I consider it worth while."

She sighed. "It is absolutely impossible for me to think of you as a chauffeur. You have the manners of a prince."

"Most princes have very bad manners, I assure you."

"I mean a very nice prince."

"You are very kind."

"Now listen," she said. "I was doing extra work at Mammoth to-day. The director of the picture on which I was working is a very decent sort and I know him. I told him about you. I said you were just the man to play the king in that film based upon the story of the King of Berania."

"I am very sorry. I told you I was not interested."

"Surely," she said tartly, "you are not such a fool as to turn down ten times what you are earning."

He shook his head. "I am afraid I am just such a fool."

"Oh, you are exasperating. I only want to help you."

"I appreciate it, but my decision is final."

"Perhaps," she said with a suspicion of reproach, "you don't consider picture acting respectable."

"On the contrary. I happen to have strong reasons."

They had long since left Hollywood and Beverly Hills and were riding along a wide paved boulevard which twisted and turned and imperceptibly climbed toward the Santa Monica Mountains. It was dimly lighted and, compared to the direct boulevards, but little traversed.

Carl had been subconsciously aware that a big car was coming along behind him, for its headlights intermittently were reflected upon his windshield. This car now signaled that it was going to pass and he swung over toward the side of the road to give it plenty of room.

The car passed close and then cut in so abruptly that Carl was obliged to turn into the shallow ditch and apply his brakes. The other car instantly came to a stop, blocking his progress.

"Hey, Decker!" called a man from the big car.

"Yes," Carl answered in surprise.

"That's him all right," he heard somebody say. Immediately two men sprang out of the car and came toward him, followed by a third.

"What is the meaning of this?" Carl demanded.

"Get out of that car," shouted the man in the lead. "We want to talk to you,"

"It's a holdup! Get away!" exclaimed the girl tensely.

"They knew my name. We have nothing to attract robbers."

The two men were standing by the door of the roadster.

"Come on, get down," commanded one of them.

"No, no, don't," pleaded Dalma. "They are terrible men."

"Do we have to drag you out?" asked the spokesman menacingly.

"What do you want?"

"We're going to beat the life out of you."

CARL'S right hand dropped from his gear shift and touched the stout cane which the girl had brought along. His eyes sparkled. He threw open the door and, cane in hand, sprang lightly upon the pavement. The nearest man swung a huge fist at him, but Carl, on his toes, sprang back like a Russian dancer and the cane came into position like a foil.

Dalma opened her pretty mouth and emitted a scream which could be heard for blocks.

"Get him quick. She'll have the cops on us," shouted the driver of the big car.

The three closed in on Carl who retreated. Feet at right angles, right knee and right arm bent, Carl waited.

"Get that stick away from him," somebody ordered.

Left foot firm on the asphalt, Carl plunged his body forward. His right arm straightened and the point of the cane was thrust into the stomach of the antagonist in front of him. The man's breath was driven from his body and he went over backward.

"Look out," shrieked Dalma.

Another antagonist rushed in from his right, and Carl, recovering with lightning rapidity, cut with his cane like a saber and it smashed viciously full against the face of his opponent. He darted back as the man on his left, wielding a short loaded club, swung for his head. The blow missed and struck his left arm so hard he thought a bone must be broken. He returned to first fencing position, thrust again with all his force and jabbed the blackjack operator where his belt should have been.

The first man was up and was drawing a gun from his pocket. As he lifted it the cane swung against his fingers with cruel impact and the gun went flying toward the other side of the road. The man who had been hit in the face had drawn a blackjack, and the original operator was about to try again.

The fellow who had drawn the gun was howling with pain, and shaking his injured hand. Dalma's screams rent the night air with their staccato. Carl withdrew to keep both opponents in front of him, his cane ready. The pair were facing the best swordsman of Europe had they but known it. There was a confident smile on his lips and a warlike glitter in his eyes.

The two rushed in together. As Carl thrust, the fellow at whom he aimed tried to grasp the stick, but a deft twist of the wrist caused it to evade his hand and to drive against his nose with dire results.

The second man was upon him, however, and then Dalma saw an exemplification of an art little known in America. Too late to bring the cane into action, Carl turned away from his enemy, bent forward, and then his left foot was driven up with irresistible power and the heel of his shoe jammed against the jaw of the thug. The man went down and completely out for the time being.

And now a police siren was heard. The two men who were able to walk, abandoned the battle, rushed to the unconscious rascal, lifted him and ran with him to their car which immediately made off.

Carl climbed back into the roadster, flexing his left arm. It hurt, but it was not broken.

A MOTORCYCLE, gleaming white, came swinging round a curve below, and with a rattle and roar drew up beside them.

"Where's the woman who was yelling?" demanded the policeman. "You?"

"Yes," said Dalma who pressed Carl's arm warningly.

"What's the trouble?"

"We almost had a crash," she said swiftly. "And the men in

the other car got out and were threatening to beat this gentleman. They said it was his fault, but it wasn't."

"Is that all?" asked the officer, laughing. "What became of
them?"

"They heard your siren, jumped in their car and drove off."

"What kind of car was it?"

"A big black one."

"Well, I'll see if I can overtake them," he said. "No damage
done to either car?"

"No, sir."

"Okay," he said and rattled away.

"Why on earth did you lie to him?" asked Carl slowly:

"Because he would have taken our names and they would
have been published in the papers, and it would probably have
meant more trouble for both of us. You were absolutely marvelous. You handled that cane exactly as Maître Morini would
have handled a sword. You beat three pugilists single-handed."

"Maître Morini, the greatest swordsman who ever lived. How
on earth do you happen to know about him?" he asked, astonished.

"My father knew him years ago in Europe."

"Morini taught me how to fence," he said. "Was your father
a swordsman?"

"When he was young, he was."

"Well, well, we must be getting on; are you so shaken you
want me to take you home?"

She pulled herself together. "No, I want our ride. But let's
go back to town and ride out in another direction. We might
meet them again."

"I believe they are through for the evening," he replied, but,
obediently, he swung the little car about and started back toward
Beverly Hills. "Why do you suppose they attacked me and how
did they know my name?"

She touched his arm gently. "You are a man," she said. "I

knew that last night, but you have demonstrated it again. You are stupid, though. Junior Swasey hired them to follow and get you."

"Impossible."

"Not at all. There are a lot of contemptible people who are rich and influential out here and this is their favorite way of getting even. Not so long ago the wife of a very big producer fell in love with a handsome young actor. Her husband was too cowardly to attack the man himself, so he hired a band of thugs who broke into the actor's house and beat him so badly that he was in the hospital for months and he was so disfigured that he can never play leads again."

"One must travel to learn," said Carl. "That harks back to the Middle Ages, though they used knives instead of clubs occasionally."

"Most likely, Junior followed you to-night and when he found that you were going to take me riding, he sent those wretches after us."

"Before I leave the Swaseys." said Carl thoughtfully, "I must have another interview with Junior."

"Don't quarrel with him, please. He can make worse trouble for you than this."

"I have a notion that I can take care of myself."

"For my sake," she pleaded. "He could easily frame you and have you sent to jail. That is done a lot out here."

"Let's dismiss the incident from our minds and talk about us," he proposed.

CHAPTER XIII

JERVIS LOSES AN ALLY

THE TRANSCONTINENTAL EXPRESS was held for five minutes while Yates sent the local police in pursuit of the murderer in the motor car. At the end of that time, the secret service man swung on board the train and made his way to Jervis's drawing room. He found the Pullman conductor making arrangements to transfer Will to quarters minus a broken window.

Will was moved to the car behind.

"Well," said Yates, "got any explanation of that?"

"What's yours?" countered Will.

"Gosh, I haven't time to figure it out. This is the second attempt on your life within a couple of weeks. Same people, eh?"

"I suppose so."

"What are they after you for?"

"Well, you may scout at my theory. What do you know about the man in New York whom the papers say is the King of Berania?"

"Just know he isn't. Some smart fellow who knows there's a lot of graft in pretending to be."

"In my opinion he is an agent of the Beranian government."

"What's he got to do with trying to have you murdered?"

"Because I am probably the only man in America who knows positively that he isn't King Carlos."

Will then told in full detail of the affray with Grandez in

his apartment in New York and the theory he had formed from it.

"Of course they hoped to find out from me where Carlos was hiding, but their main object was to put me out of the way so that I couldn't expose the impostor."

"The assistant secretary told me he was a faker and not to bother about him, but to locate the real king."

"I wonder how he knew."

"He didn't say. I took it for granted he was some grifter, but it looks as though he has some kind of gang behind him."

"I had no notion that they would make another attempt on my life on the way to Los Angeles, because I figured that they expected me to lead them to Carlos. That's why I was so ready to believe that Mlle. LeFevre was sent along to keep an eye on me."

YATES shook his head. "Trying to figure out how the other fellow's mind works is a bigger gamble than playing roulette."

"They must have agents all over the country,"

"What probably happened," said Yates, "if the Beranians are responsible for this, is that they got a line on a big shot in New York, gave him your drawing room letter and car number and a bundle of jack and he wired to friends out this way to check you out."

"But I can't understand why."

"Any other people anxious to read about your funeral?"

"I'm sure there aren't. I've been out of America for three years. I never had any enemies."

"Not insured heavily in favor of anybody?" asked Yates, grinning.

"I'm an orphan. I have very little insurance and my little fortune goes, when I die, to an old maid cousin who is a church member."

"All right. There is nothing to stop you coming back from Los Angeles to expose this phony king."

"No."

"Well, that's probably it."

"But they want me to lead them to Carlos."

"Maybe they don't need you as much as you think. They are not supporting this Humpty Dumpty in New York to give him a good time. They are planning to pull something big and don't want you to spoil it. Mind if I move into the drawing room with you?"

"There's plenty of room."

"Looks to me as though you were in more danger than King Carlos," commented the secret service man. "Here's hoping they don't wreck the train."

"Denver papers," announced the porter, thrusting his head into the drawing room. "Come aboard at the last station. You gents want a couple? Ain't no charge."

"I'll take anything that's free," smiled the detective. "Thank you, George."

He tossed a copy of the Denver *Post* to Jervis and opened one himself.

"Well, well!" he exclaimed. "We can't seem to get away from Berania."

Jervis opened his paper.

REVOLT FLARES IN SOUTHERN BERANIA

That was the headline. Under a Madrova date line was the following dispatch:

> The Duke of Burzio, who managed to escape from prison through connivance of his jailers, so the authorities believe, has raised the royal standard in Southern Berania. He appeared three days ago in Sepoia, the largest city in the South, held a meeting with military leaders, and the army division quartered there went over to the royal cause. Peasant volunteers are flocking in by the thousands. The peasants claim they never wanted the king driven out, but were deceived by the republicans. As famine has been stalking through the country

districts of the South and the republic has been unable to alleviate it through lack of funds, the disaffection seems to be general.

From the Palace, President Torres has issued a statement that the revolt is purely local and will be sternly suppressed. Troop movements south are under way. It is anticipated that, if the revolt makes headway, King Carlos, who is supposed to be in America, will return and place himself at the head of his supporters.

"**SORT** of bears out your theory regarding the danger Carlos is in," said Yates. "I'm all in favor of a republic myself, having voted the straight Democratic ticket for twenty years. If I were true to my principles I suppose I ought to stand aside and let them get this king."

"My dear fellow, the people of Berania have no more voice in this fake republic than the people of Russia have in the Communist government. It was set up as the result of a conspiracy between military traitors and politicians. They told the people that everybody would have a chicken in the pot and unlimited bread and cheese if the republic was established, and having kept none of their promises, the people are tired of being fooled. Berania is the sort of country that has to have a king."

"And if Carlos is murdered there is nobody to take his place?"

"Not a soul. He is the last of the royal line."

"By George! The scheme is to kill Carlos and take this actor in New York to Berania and stick him on the throne, eh?"

"They wouldn't dare. Too many people in Madrova know the real monarch."

"Well, this rebellion will make them try harder to get rid of the lad."

"Of course."

"I think he'd be a sucker to go back. This is the greatest country in the world."

Will laughed. "He told me once that the king business was

the only way he knew to make a living. He's ready to return if they really want him."

"I hope he leaves America soon."

"So do I," said Jervis. "I'll introduce you to Mlle. LeFevre and ask you to give me your candid opinion regarding her."

"And you hope like hell I'll give her a clean bill of health."

Will nodded. "It will about break my heart if you don't."

"I'm going to check up on a few things," said Yates. "See you in a little while."

During his absence Will made a second inspection of his luggage but found nothing else missing. His search occupied ten minutes and Yates was back as he completed it. Yates wore a crestfallen expression.

"I am afraid I went off half cocked when I sent back the telegram to stop that woman," he admitted. "In fact I know I did. She is still on the train."

"What!" exclaimed Jervis joyfully.

The detective nodded. "And she does not use 'Cœur d'Eros' perfume. I encountered her in the aisle, stumbled against her on purpose and got her into conversation. She is an American who lives on a ranch in Wyoming."

"Then who on earth did break into my luggage?"

Yates looked uncomfortable. "I regret to report," he said slowly, "that Mlle. LeFevre is no longer on the train."

"What!" exclaimed Will in astonishment and distress.

"She alighted at Newton. The train was held five minutes, so that it is unlikely that she could have missed it unintentionally."

"Are you sure she isn't on the train? Perhaps she is in a compartment with Goldsmith."

"His door is open. He is alone. I talked with the porter of her car who remembered helping her down the steps."

"I—I can't believe it."

"The only indication that she may have been left behind accidentally is that her suitcases remain in her section."

"Ah, that's different. Of course it was an accident."

"Or she hoped it would appear to be an accident," said Yates dryly. "It's a pity that you did not recognize her perfume."

"But you said yourself that she could not possibly have gone into my drawing room."

"That's a fact. I was watching her, but, now that I think of it, I went into the smoking compartment long enough to smoke a cigarette."

"You're a hell of a detective," said Will disgustedly.

YATES shrugged.

"You remember that I had no object in watching her. She was not under suspicion."

"All right. She went through my luggage, and left by prearrangement at the station where a plot to murder me was arranged, which means she was in the plot. I don't believe it, Yates."

"Well," replied the detective, "I don't know the lady as well as you do. I was so certain that it wasn't her, that I took it for granted that the woman in the car back had done the job and got off at the previous station. Of course, I would have made sure that she wasn't on the train if we hadn't made that last stop before I had a chance. I'm taking possession of her bags and sending them up to the baggage car to examine them at my leisure."

"Have them brought here. I know better than you what will be incriminating."

"That's right. I'll have the porter bring them right in."

He vanished, to return followed by a porter carrying two suitcases.

Will watched Yates deftly pick the lock of a stylish black leather suitcase.

"She has a couple of trunks in the baggage car," he stated. "I'll go through them later. Now let's see what she's got. Ah!"

He lifted from its nest in pink French lingerie an Italian leather box, unlocked, which proved to contain perfume.

"Ah," he said again. "Cœur d'Eros. Smell this."

He held under Will's nose the little bottle which gave forth a sweet pungent and indescribable scent.

"That's what she was wearing, is it not?"

"No," declared Will, "it certainly is not. I'm afraid we're making a terrible mistake."

"Oh, no harm done. What perfume did she have on?"

"I didn't really notice any."

"You're a great help. Even if she's guilty, you don't want to believe it. Right?"

"I guess so," Will admitted shamefacedly.

With the skill of experience in investigation, Yates went through the suitcase, which, however, contained nothing but lingerie, *froufrous*, knick-knacks and trinkets, all of which bore the stamp of Paris manufacture.

"No help there," pronounced Yates, who proceeded to open the second suitcase. This contained nothing but two neatly folded traveling dresses, three nightgowns, and three pairs of dainty French shoes. No letters, no papers, no documents— nothing in the least helpful.

"Looks as though she knew we would learn nothing from what she left behind," said Yates. "Well, nothing like being thorough. I'm going up forward to the baggage car and go through the trunks."

"Any chance of her overtaking the train?"

"Not unless she takes an aëroplane, and that town is not a landing place."

"Poor kid. If she's innocent, she's in a terrible state," Will said gloomily.

"She'll hop the next train, three hours behind us, and get to

Los Angeles six or eight hours after us, if she's what she claims to be. Might as well lunch before I tackle the trunks."

"I'm not hungry."

Yates laughed. "I'll eat for two," he promised.

HE WAS gone two hours, time employed by Will in gazing gloomily out at the dreary landscape. When Yates returned he wore a curious expression and held in his hand a sheet of yellow paper.

"Find anything in the trunks?" asked Will eagerly.

"Nothing that sheds any light. A whole library of French books, but no letters. Clothes enough to open a dress shop in Hollywood and an autographed photograph, probably spurious, of the King of Berania."

"What?"

"Looks like a rubber stamp autograph. One of the kind they sell in stationery shops over there. Point is, Mr. Jervis, I've got to leave you. Received a radio-telegraph message from Washington ten minutes ago at that last station."

He passed it over. Will ran his eye over the message.

> Following false scent. Return to New York immediately.
> DOWNES.

"What on earth does it mean?" he demanded.

"You can search me. I'll drop off at a flag station and hop the next express back East."

"I don't understand this at all."

"I don't have to understand it. Orders are orders."

"A 'false scent.' You started West because you thought Carlos was in Los Angeles."

"Right."

"Well, he is. I know it. He wrote me from there."

"Since he wrote you he may have jumped back to New York. That faker may have got his goat."

"In which case Downes would have couched his message

differently. Look here, remain on the train to Albuquerque to-morrow morning, and I'll get him on long distance. I'll stay over a train if necessary."

"Brother, I belong to an organization that jumps when they push the button. I'm leaving at once. Orders are orders,"

"Have you considered that this may be a fake message?"

"There is a certain word used which identifies it. Guess the State Department knows more than we do."

"Well," said Jervis sadly, "I'll be sorry to see you go. I'll still stop off at Albuquerque and phone Downes. I may be able to persuade him to turn you back."

"You hope you'll find the French girl on the train behind this one."

"Well," admitted Jervis, "yes."

"I hope no woman ever gets me into that state of mind. I hate having to quit you, Jervis. You certainly need a guardian; besides which, they may be framing more surprises for you."

"I'm warned, and I'm careful from now on."

"Well, I'll have to hunt up the conductor and arrange to have the train stopped. Best of luck."

"Good-by," said Jervis regretfully. "Mark my words, you'll come back flying."

"Hope so. I'd like to see a little more of your French girl myself."

Left alone, Jervis locked his door and abandoned himself to gloomy reflections. *Mademoiselle* would have made things interesting during the remainder of the trip. Yates would have been a tower of strength. Well, he would get Washington on the long distance from Albuquerque and try to find out why the detective had been taken off a job upon which he was badly needed.

CHAPTER XIV

A KING GIVES AUDIENCE

IN THE DRAWING room of the New York hotel suite occupied by the individual known as Alfonso Gomez there was an animated scene at the moment when an assassin in Nebraska was shooting at Will Jervis through a train window.

In a very large and comfortable armchair sat Gomez, the man who was masquerading as King Carlos of Berania. Beside him stood his secretary, an oily person who spoke English with a strong Beranian accent.

Facing him, hats in hand, endeavoring to appear respectful in the presence of royalty, stood half a dozen newspaper reporters, and two men with cameras loafed near the door awaiting their moment.

"I have arranged this interview with Señor Gomez at the request of you journalists," said the secretary. "You have his permission to ask him questions, but him you will excuse if he does not choose to answer them."

"Your majesty—" began Bill Oakes of the *Tribune.*

"One moment," interrupted the secretary. "You must not address him as 'your majesty.'"

"I beg your pardon. Señor Gomez, we want to respect your incognito, but a serious situation has arisen, and a statement from you will be much appreciated by the New York newspapers. Are you going back to head the royalist revolt?"

"I will answer you this way. If I were King Carlos, I would not return. I am very happy here. Your New York is wonderful.

Your theaters are sublime, your women are marvelous." He smacked his lips.

"Is it true that you escaped with the crown jewels?" asked the reporter eagerly.

"That I do not answer."

"But you have investments of fifty millions in the United States."

"I have enough," said the pretender significantly.

"But if people are fighting to restore you to the throne?"

"They are fools," he said contemptuously. "The republican troops will soon crush this silly revolt."

"After all," said Davis of the *Journal,* "they are fighting for you, and you ought to have some sympathy for them."

"I am a simple Beranian gentleman," Gomez replied, "and since I have seen your glorious United States I am converted to republicanism. The era of kings is over."

"Maybe they'd let you go back if they knew you had become a republican," suggested a reporter.

"I shall never go back," declared Gomez. "I will confide in you, gentlemen. I do not like Berania. It has a bad climate. Its capital is a stupid village. Its palaces are not to be compared with your hotels. Its people are ignorant and bigoted. They are five hundred years behind the times. I consider they did me a great favor by establishing the republic, and if they have to use cannon and machine guns to maintain it, I hope they use them efficiently."

"Wow!" exclaimed one of the reporters. "Hot stuff!"

Gomez posed for several photographs, drinks were served, and the newspaper men departed to gather near the telephone booths in the hotel lobby.

"As an interview, that was a darb," said Oakes thoughtfully. "As a man, this king is about an inch tall."

"A dirty polecat," declared Davis. "Here are these poor people getting killed for him, and he sneers at them."

"Well," said Oakes, "the cables will sizzle. Can you imagine the poor duke down in Sepoia when he reads how the king feels about things. And the noble peasants when they hear that they are ignorant, bigoted and stupid? That rebellion is just the same as busted this minute."

"The whole thing is very curious," said Davis slowly. "If we publish his statement verbatim, I think we are doing exactly what he wishes. From what Will Jervis told me about Carlos, he's a swell guy and the last man in the world to issue such a disgraceful statement."

"New York has ruined him," replied Oakes, with a laugh. "After all, Jervis didn't know him very well. Just flew him from Madrova to Paris."

"I have a hunch," said Davis hesitatingly, "that this fellow is phony. If he was working for the republic, he couldn't serve them better. I'd like to have a talk with Jervis, but I can't let myself get scooped."

BACK in the apartment of Señor Gomez, that worthy and his secretary were conversing briskly in their own language.

"It succeeded to a marvel," said the secretary. "The fools drank it as a cat drinks cream. What is it, Francisco?"

A valet had entered.

"There is a man outside who says he represents the government of the United States," the man reported.

The pair exchanged apprehensive glances and then the secretary laughed.

"We are ready for him," he declared. "Admit him."

There entered a heavily built, solid-jawed man.

"Inspector Briggs, United States Secret Service," he said. "Which of you gentlemen is King Carlos of Berania?"

"Neither of us," replied Gomez quickly.

"Well, you're the fellow the newspapers claim is this king, ain't you?"

"If the newspapers wish to honor me, is it my fault? I have

denied to them again and again that I am his majesty, but they refuse to believe me."

"Well, I believe you," said Inspector Briggs. "Who the devil are you?"

"Sir," said the secretary, bristling, "your manner is offensive."

"Now that's too bad. You're a Beranian, ain't you, Mr. Gomez?"

"Between ourselves and in strict confidence, yes."

"How did you get into this country?"

Gomez smiled. "Through a chink in your immigration laws, my friend. I refer you to the State Department at Washington."

The inspector grinned. "I just came from there with special instructions. Let's see your passport."

"With pleasure," replied Gomez. "Fetch it, Francisco."

The valet went into the bedchamber and returned with a little red book which he handed to his master. Gomez passed it on to Briggs.

The inspector opened it and his astonishment caused the Beranians to exchange amused glances.

"Carl Decker," Briggs said aloud. "Say, I guess there has been a misunderstanding. Tell you what happened, sir," said the inspector eagerly. "When you were slipped through the immigration lines, I was assigned to keep an eye on you for your protection. Next thing I knew you moved out without leaving an address and I couldn't trace you."

"I assure you I have not tried to conceal myself," said Gomez indifferently.

"I got bawled out by the department and they put another man on the job. This fellow thought he had trailed you to the Grand Central where you bought a ticket for California under an assumed name and he hot-footed out there.

"But to-day I got orders to round you up. The department thought you were tied up in some way with this Beranian that tried to shoot up Mr. William Jervis and I was to give you the works. The passport clears you, though."

"Your government is rather suspicious, it seems to me," said Gomez with hauteur.

"It was all the fault of this colleague of mine," apologized Briggs. "I had a good look at you when you first came to town and I can go on the stand and swear you're the same man."

AFTER the government man had made his exit the two conspirators could hardly restrain their jubilation.

"I wonder if his majesty has missed his passport," said Gomez.

"In a very short time it would be of no use to him," said the secretary significantly. "The phone!"

He picked up the instrument.

"Ah," he said, and then he listened intently.

The false king saw his face lengthen.

"It is too bad," he said finally. "We must begin over again."

"What is it?" demanded Gomez anxiously.

"That accursed Jervis bears a charmed life. The attempt was made two hours ago. The bullets missed their mark and one of those damned Americans who are dead shots killed our agent."

Gomez swore fluently. "He and Carlos are now our only peril."

"Carlos is nothing. The rat lurks in his hole, but Jervis must be removed and at once. With him out of the way we are all set. Nothing has been overlooked. It was our luck that Carlos evaded that fool of a government spy. He is now convinced that you are the Aronhof."

"I am an Aronhof—"

"With the bar sinister," modified the secretary. "Everything dovetails nicely. The sentiments you expressed to the reporters should gratify the American government, republican as it is, and they will settle the Duke of Burzio. And your arrival in Los Angeles to appear in the film may be the means of putting Carlos within our reach. That is something the pride of the Aronhof will not be able to stomach.

"It may be that we shall catch him and Jervis together and kill two birds with one stone."

"In the meantime," said the pretender, yawning, "there are two young ladies of the chorus coming here this afternoon. Have we enough champagne?"

"Francisco will attend to that."

"Do you not envy me my position?" demanded Gomez, laughing.

"Well," replied the secretary slowly, "perhaps. I, however, am not a half-brother and double of King Carlos."

CHAPTER XV

A RATTLESNAKE STRIKES

THE TELEPHONE AWAKENED the man who no longer had a passport to justify the use of the name Carl Decker at seven thirty in the morning. The king sprang lightly out of bed and took up the receiver. The butler was calling.

"Mrs. Swasey wants you to present yourself in her study immediately after breakfast," said the butler. "She left the order last night. Looks as though you were in for a bunch of trouble, Decker."

"Thank you for telling me. I'll report," Carl said quietly. Junior, of course, had trumped up some tale, and he was about to be discharged. He did not care. The job was becoming uncomfortable.

The condemned man ate a hearty breakfast, his mind busy with the singular pleasure of his excursion with Dalma Dawning last evening. His state of mind toward Miss Dawning had clarified during the night. He was in love with her, and he wanted to marry her. Never fascinated by the life of a king, he detested it now.

He told himself that he owed no duty to Berania. The nation had kicked him out and absolved him from all allegiance. He was under no obligation to hold himself in readiness for the remote possibility of a recall. The republic might endure, or collapse, for all of him.

After all, the Beranians were no more benighted than the inhabitants of various South American and East European

*He stared unsuspectingly
at the paper.*

republics, and eventually the honest republicans would throw
the rascals out and govern honestly.

What he proposed to do was to get some sort of employment
by which he could support Dalma, marry her, and live the life
of an American citizen in happy obscurity.

It was marvelous to be free to marry the girl you loved. It
was sublime to be a resident of a country not constantly in a
turmoil. He and his bride would settle down in some quiet
suburb of this city so delightfully situated in California, and
the world would never know what had become of Carlos of
Berania.

And he had resources. In his possession were jewels, his
personal property, worth thirty or forty thousand dollars. They
were jewels hallowed in Berania by association with past generations of Aronhofs, historic mementoes like the ruby presented to his grandfather by the Pope, and the diamond-stud-
ded penknife sent to himself before the World War by the
Kaiser. There was the miniature of his great-aunt Lydia with
the huge emerald at its base, and the five carat blue diamond

in a solitaire ring which his father had given him twenty years ago.

If he hadn't been a fool he would have taken the other valuable trinkets in his bedchamber when he abdicated, for he could have realized enough on them to live in California for a lifetime without labor; but how was he to know that he would fall in love with a little American picture actress and settle down contentedly in a remote American city? At the moment of his flight he expected to be brought back to his throne by popular demand in a month or two.

He was confident that Dalma was in love with him. The way she had squeezed his arm as he drove along after the encounter with the ruffians on Beverly Boulevard! He had been given the opportunity upon two occasions to play a heroic rôle before her, and that, with a woman, is worth months of wooing.

There was a contented smile on Carl's lips and his eyes were bright when he stood before the enormously wealthy widow who employed him. Mrs. Mason Swasey was sitting at her desk in her study when he entered. It was her practice to go over her own accounts and pay all her bills with personal checks, and she had never employed a secretary or a steward. As she was not a deft penwoman, she found this hard labor, but she had learned in her youth to be thrifty and she had never got over it.

"**HOW** are you, Decker?" she said briskly, "What's the trouble between you and my boy?"

"What does he say, madam?" countered the chauffeur.

"He says you're incompetent, surly, and disrespectful."

Carl bit his lower lip to conceal a smile.

"Specifically, what does he allege, madam?"

"Humph! You drove him night before last?"

"Yes, madam."

"What happened?"

"I'm sorry, madam. I must refer you to him."

"Well," she said with a sigh, "it's my opinion that you are a very decent lad and a good chauffeur, I've no fault to find with you at all."

"Thank you, madam."

"But I'm going to fire you just the same. Kind of a dirty trick."

Carl bowed.

"Junior didn't come right out and accuse you of anything," she added. "But I have my suspicions. It ain't on his account I'm getting rid of you."

"Perhaps you will satisfy my curiosity."

She leaned back, folded her hands upon her ample stomach and smiled at him kindly.

"You're too young, too good looking and too gentlemanly to be working around this place," she said. "I'm firing you because my daughter Gladys praises you too much."

"Madam!" he exclaimed. Secretly he was amused by her frankness.

"I don't accuse you of making up to her," she added. "But you might be. You foreigners are sly and you don't care where the money comes from so long as you get it. I'm just nipping this thing in the bud. And I want to tell you, young man, that my daughter hasn't a penny to bless herself with. I've got all the money, and if she doesn't do what I tell her she'll never get a cent of it."

"Mrs. Swasey," said Carl frigidly, "I am not in the least interested in the financial affairs of you and your daughter. I am dismissed. There is no more to be said. Good morning."

He turned away.

"Now wait a minute!" she exclaimed. "I know I'm treating you rotten. You probably haven't done a thing you shouldn't. You're just playing in hard luck, but a fellow like you won't have any trouble getting another job. I'll give you the highest recommendations."

"I don't care for references from you, Mrs. Swasey," Carl said coldly.

"And I'm going to give you two months' wages. That's pretty good, ain't it? You'll be working again in a couple of days. Here."

She extended a slip of pink paper and looked up at him. Mrs. Swasey was a stolid woman with no imagination, but when she looked at the man, chills crept up and down her spine, her heart began to beat faster, her color faded and she felt an impulse to grovel at his feet.

The figure fronting her seemed to grow before her eyes. Carlos looked down on her as from a great height. His face was transfigured; the great luminous eyes penetrated to her marrow. For the first time in twenty years she felt as insignificant as she had been in the days when she knocked at people's back doors and asked for washing.

Carl took the check from her hand, tore it into small pieces and laid the fragments upon her desk.

"Good day, madam," he said in a tone which cut her like a knife. He strode from the room. Mrs. Swasey felt tears rolling down her cheeks. She suffered as though she had been snubbed by a society leader.

CARL left the house, a great weight lifted from his shoulders. He wanted to tear off the livery and present himself to Dalma, a free man. What did he care about the miserable check for two months' wages? What had he been thinking of to have placed himself in a position where he could be patronized by a vulgar woman when he had a respectable competence in his possession?

So completely had his point of view changed since last night that he could not understand now why he had been ready to accept employment as a servant when he could have sold the baubles for enough to live on. Yet, until he met Dalma, King Carlos would have starved before he would have pawned a single one of those precious relics of bis kingdom. Now, he did not consider them of the slightest consequence. He would dispose of them all without a qualm.

"Carl," said a soft voice. He looked up. Gladys Swasey had come out of the rose garden and intercepted him.

"Good morning," he said stiffly.

"What did mother want to see you for?" she demanded.

"To tell me that I am no longer in her employ."

"Oh!" gasped Gladys. "What an outrage! That scoundrel Junior—"

"I don't think your brother affected her decision, Miss Swasey."

"Of course he did. I'll fix him. Don't let this bother you at all. I'll see mother right away. I won't permit her to discharge you."

"Please, Miss Swasey, do not interfere. I was about to resign."

"Why? You won't find a nicer place. I promise you that Junior won't annoy you any more. I'll attend to that."

"I'm sorry, but I prefer to go."

Gladys grew pale and Carl turned his eyes away. He was in love himself and he was very sorry for the fine young woman before him.

"Then you want to go," she said in a low tone.

"Yes," he said. "It is better so."

"You mustn't think of yourself as a chauffeur," she said swiftly. "I know that you are a gentleman in distress. I have no doubt you come of a better family than I do. I like you, Carl. I want to be friends. Mother doesn't understand. Please stay."

"Miss Swasey," he said gravely. "I will tell you why I am leaving. I am in love with a young lady who does not wish me to be a chauffeur."

He met her fine eyes firmly. Tears sprang into them and then she stepped aside.

"I did not understand," she said softly. "Of course you must do as she wishes. I hope you will be very happy."

"Thank you, miss," he said affecting not to comprehend what she was revealing. "Good morning."

"You are leaving at once?"

"Yes, Miss Swasey."

She put out her hand. "Then good-by."

They shook hands and he continued on to the garage and climbed to his quarters. To his astonishment, they were occupied.

Sitting on his bed was a big man smoking a cigar. On a straight-backed chair was a little man, also smoking a cigar. At the window stood Junior Swasey with a malicious smile on his face.

"What does this mean?" asked Carl angrily.

The big man rose and removed his cigar.

"You're under arrest, mister," he said curtly.

Carl looked beyond him and saw one of his bags lying open on the bed. Another was open on the floor beyond.

"With what am I charged?" he asked quietly.

"Robbery," snapped Junior Swasey. "Murder too, for all I know."

"And whom did I rob?" asked Carl calmly.

"We don't have to answer questions. Do you come quietly or shall I put on the bracelets?" inquired the big man.

DELIBERATELY Carl stepped to the chair upon which the little man was sitting, tipped him off and sat down.

"Neither," he said evenly. "You'll make an explanation of this outrage here and now."

"I'll tell you," said Junior, who was spoiling to gloat. "I suspected you of being some kind of crook right along. I telephoned the police, brought them here and authorized them to go through your luggage. We found plenty."

"Then these gentlemen are of the Los Angeles police?" asked the king.

"You bet your life," snarled the little man, who naturally resented having been spilled upon the floor.

"I am glad to hear that," replied Carl. "I thought you might be some of the scoundrels Swasey sent out last night to thrash me. You have a search warrant, of course?"

The big man looked at the little man. "What do you think of that for gall?"

"Beats everything," stated the little man.

"Let's get going," said the big man, "You coming peaceably, feller?"

"Not until I have an answer to my question."

The big man whipped out a gun and covered the chauffeur.

"Only one way to talk with crooks," he growled, "Get up out of there or I'll drill you."

Carl laughed easily. "I am not afraid of your popgun. You dare not shoot, my friend. Suppose you answer my question."

"Can you beat that?" demanded the little man as though witnessing a marvel.

With an exasperated laugh the big detective restored his gun.

"All right," he said. "I'll answer. We haven't got a search warrant. You might make trouble for us only what we found justified us in exceeding our authority."

Carl arched his eyebrows.

"And what did you find?"

"Only about fifty thousand dollars' worth of loot: diamonds and rubies and emeralds."

"And what makes you believe they were stolen?"

"It stands to reason. You're a chauffeur, ain't you? You make a hundred and fifty a month. Where would you get this stuff if you didn't swipe it?"

"I believe it is your business to answer that question. The jewels are my personal property. You will kindly leave this room."

"What's the matter with you two boobs?" demanded Junior angrily. "Handcuff him and drag him off. Knock him on the head if he resists."

"We'll find out quick enough who you stole 'em from," said the detective, ignoring Junior. "We hold them until we find the owner. And we lock you up so the judge won't have to look for you when he gives you twenty years."

"Is this what you call justice in America?"

"None of your lip, you damned foreigner. How long you been in this country?"

"About six months."

"Where's your passport?"

"In that larger bag."

"No it ain't. We've been through it and we can't find no passport. By gosh, Jack, that's the charge. Illegal entry into the United States. We'll pinch him on that and jail him till we find who owns these sparklers."

FOR THE first time Carl was apprehensive. Never having occasion to use his passport since his arrival in America, he was not aware that it had been stolen from him in New York.

"I think I should like to talk to your superior officers," he said slowly. "I shall go with you. Permit me to inform you that I have a complete inventory of the gems in my luggage and it will go hard with you if they are not all produced at police headquarters."

"Don't you worry about that, brother," said the big man, grinning good naturedly, The attitude of the chauffeur had perplexed and a little perturbed him until he had found a plausible excuse for placing him under arrest.

As Carl was leaving the room with the detectives, Junior could not resist a parting gibe.

"I told you I'd get even," he jeered.

Carl did not bother to reply. He was wondering what had become of his passport and chiding himself that he had not placed his jewels in a bank vault in Los Angeles as he had done in New York. The situation was serious, but not in the way which Junior and the policemen supposed. All he had to do was to proclaim his identity and they would have to release him; but, to announce himself as King of Berania would be to notify the Beranian agents where he might be found, a thing he must not do except as a last resource.

Besides, the pride of the Aronhofs would not permit him to allow the world to know that King Carlos had donned the livery of a menial, and he had seen enough of American newspapers to know how that episode would appeal to them. And his recognition as the exiled monarch would play havoc with his plans to win and wed Dalma Dawning, despite the handicap of his having been a servant, and to live with her in contented obscurity.

Of course Dalma would accept the hand of Carlos of Berania. So would any ambitious girl, and he knew that she was very ambitious. He didn't want her that way. He wanted her to fall into the arms of Carl Decker, ex-chauffeur.

It was a horrible dilemma and curiously enough, in considering it, Carl did not give a thought to the possibility that it might be complicated by the mountebank in New York, nor did it occur to him that his double might have established himself firmly by a display of the stolen passport.

He rode silently ten or twelve miles into the center of Los Angeles, a captor on either side of him in the tonneau of the big car which Clancy was driving stolidly, though he was probably eaten up with curiosity to know what had happened to his fellow chauffeur.

Halfway down town, Carl saw a way out. Will Jervis was in New York recovering from his wound. Jervis, he was aware, had influence with the State Department at Washington. The way he had made arrangements for the king's secret admission to the United States proved that. Jervis was his friend. Jervis could go to the government, explain the situation, and word would come from Washington that the prisoner was all right and must be released.

It might mean a few days in a jail pending action by Jervis, but that was preferable to revealing his identity, bringing down murderers upon his neck and losing his present delightful stand-ing with Dalma Dawning.

That was what he would do: send a carefully couched tele-gram to Will Jervis and that exceedingly efficient person would again come to his rescue. By the time the car reached police headquarters Carl had become so cheerful that the detectives began again to be apprehensive. What did he have up his sleeve?

CHAPTER XVI

A KING IN JAIL

CARL WAS CONDUCTED before a captain of police and left standing while the big detective poured into the captain's ears the details of his alleged crimes and backed up his statement by drawing from his pockets and placing upon the desk the articles found in the prisoner's suitcase.

The captain examined them with avid curiosity.

"Guess these jewels are real, all right," he said slowly. "And these settings are real antiques. Whoever lost them will pay a big reward for their return. How much do you think they're worth, Graham?"

"Fifty thousand if they're worth a cent."

The captain turned penetrating eyes upon the King of Berania.

"Well," he said gruffly. "What have you got to say for yourself?"

"That those articles are my property. Kindly return them to me."

The reply caused the fat and lean detectives to dissolve into mirth while the captain grinned appreciatively.

"Yeah? How come you're working as a chauffeur with a fortune in your possession?"

"Because those jewels have been in my family for generations and I do not care to sell them."

"Well, mister, I wouldn't think of contradicting you, but I'm going to mind these sparklers for you till we get a chance to send round their description. You just don't ring true to me."

Carl clenched his fists and controlled his wrath.

"Permit me to point out to you," he said, "that you have no warrant for my arrest, that no charge of theft has been made against me, that I insist that these articles found in my possession by an illegal search belong to me and I demand that they be returned to me and that I be released. I know enough about law to know that I am being unjustly treated."

The captain, who was a plump, round-faced, rosy-cheeked man with an ingenuous smile but hard eyes, leaned his elbows on his desk and studied the man before him.

"Young fellow," he said pleasantly, "you've got a kick coming, all right. These boys had no business busting into your room and going through your stuff and I certainly would hop on them except for the fact that they found fifty thousand dollars' worth of junk on a chauffeur. We cops have to do a lot of things that aren't exactly according to Hoyle in order to suppress crime in this man's town. You have a come-back, though. You can sue us for illegal arrest after you've proved that you own this stuff. I never heard of anybody collecting for that, but it's your privilege."

"The burden of the proof is on you," retorted Carl. "That's the corner stone of Anglo-Saxon justice."

The captain nodded gravely. "That's right. On the other hand, I consider you a suspicious character. Can you identify yourself and show me bills of sale for these diamonds and rubies and emeralds that are worth a barrel of money?"

Carl did not answer.

"We can't go into court and convict you of theft unless we can show from whom and how and when you swiped the stuff, but we're going to lock you up while we telegraph a description of this Jewelry around the country. I bet you ten dollars to a quarter that we learn to whom they belong in a couple of days."

"I protest against such illegal action."

"Sure you do," said the captain good-naturedly. "So do all the crooks. I'd do it myself. Anyhow, we have a right to hold you for the Federal authorities, for you're an alien and you haven't got a passport."

"Look here," pleaded Carl, "can't you tell by looking at me that I'm not a criminal?"

The captain laughed. "I quit trying to do that years ago. Take him up to the jail, boys. Tell 'em to treat him nice and hold him till we call for him."

"I wish to send a telegram to New York," said Carl, abandoning the effort to persuade these police officials to obey their own laws.

"Got the price?" asked the captain.

"Yes."

"Give the boy a telegraph blank. We aim to please."

Carl scratched off a message, and the captain held out his hand for it.

Am illegally arrested and in jail in Los Angeles. Will appreciate your good offices. Carl.

He addressed it to Will Jervis in New York City.

THE CAPTAIN read it aloud, to Carl's indignation.

"Any of you fellows know anything about this Will Jervis?" he demanded.

The little detective piped up: "A fellow by that name shot three burglars he found in his apartment in New York a few weeks ago. I remember reading it because he was the same guy that got the King of Berania out of his country when they had the revolution over there. The paper told about that, too."

"Get a file of the newspapers," commanded the captain. "I read something about that, but I didn't remember the name."

"I'll save you the trouble," said Carl. "It is the same man."

"Were you his chauffeur?"

"No; he was a friend."

"Does he know who these jewels belong to?"

"He knows they belong to me."

"What the heck do you think that guy can do for you out here?"

"I think he will convince you that you are making a grave error."

"Fine," the captain replied. "We don't claim to be infallible. Send the telegram, Graham, but scratch out that word 'illegal,' after you've taken this gent to a nice, airy cell."

"How about finger-printing him?"

"Sure, better have him photographed and finger-printed. We may find all about him in our files. Got any objection, mister?"

"I object to everything you have done to me and propose to do. I yield to force."

"Then that's all right."

Carl was taken to the record department, where he posed for pictures and had prints taken of all ten fingers. Having a remarkable gift for reconciling himself to situations, he found much to interest him in the efficient, businesslike methods of the men in charge of this department. And he was sure that his incarceration would last no longer than it took to send a telegram to New York and to phone from New York to the State Department at Washington.

After the finger-print men were through with him he was conducted into an elevator and shot skyward. The prison, it appeared, was located high up in the tower of the building.

He was unable to restrain a gasp of admiration at the view from the window of the jail office, and he noted that everything was spick and span and shining with newness. As a matter of fact, the great building was only a few years old. The best jail in Berania was two hundred and fifty years of age and as dismal as it was ancient.

As he was being held without a charge preferred against him, he was not forced to don prison clothes, but he was locked up in a small cell which was spotlessly clean and splendidly ventilated. The steel door clanged on his heels and he was left to his reflections.

They were not as bitter as might be expected. If he had remained in Berania he would have been thrust into a dungeon from which he probably would have emerged to mount the scaffold. His incarceration here would be short, and, as the police were acting illegally, there would be no publicity whatever.

What troubled him most of all was that Dalma would expect him this evening and he could send her no word without revealing that he was in jail. He did not honor the malicious junior Swasey with resentment. He had rather liked the garrulous police captain. Carl, in fact, had the advantage over common men in his consciousness of royalty. Muck could not smirch him; nothing could degrade him in his own estimation save a disgraceful act of his own.

As for the police and people of this city, they would be overwhelmed with dismay and regret if he chose to inform them of the identity of the person they were treating so scurvily.

After a few minutes he lay down upon the cot and closed his eyes. He was conscious of the bruise on his left arm from the blackjack of the ruffian whom Junior had set upon him the night before, but it did not prevent him from falling asleep in ten minutes.

CHAPTER XVII

"NOT FOR ANY PRICE!"

HIS TELEGRAM WENT humming over the wires to New York and was delivered to Jervis's apartment. The superintendent, following instructions left by Will, notified the telegraph company to send it on to a certain hotel in Los Angeles, where Will Jervis found it upon the following morning.

Jervis had checked off the train at Albuquerque, discovered that he would have to wait many hours for the train behind, and was fortunate enough to get a clear wire to the home of the Secretary of State in Washington. The connection was made in six or seven minutes and caught the Secretary as he was leaving for his office, it being a few minutes of ten in the morning in Washington.

"Jervis speaking," Will said. "Why did you recall Yates?"

"Because a certain personage is in New York," came the guarded reply.

"You are mistaken; he is in Los Angeles."

"I am not mistaken. Our man is in New York. 1 have positive proof of it."

"Do you mean that faker?"

"He is no faker. He has a passport you know about."

Will was so astonished that he almost dropped the instrument.

"Anything else?" asked the Secretary. *"I'm* late for the office."

"Yes. I've seen that fellow, and he is phony. If he has the passport, he either stole it or forged it."

"Well, we will let Yates investigate the matter."

"I assure you I need him."

"My dear Will, I can't assign secret service men to you. Have you seen the statement by this person in the morning papers? He expresses the same sentiments which you told me he had expressed to you."

"My man wouldn't be interviewed. He wouldn't express any sentiments. Can't you see—"

"At present I can't. Call me up when you have more convincing arguments."

The Secretary hung up and Will, much perplexed, left the booth. He had not yet seen the morning newspapers. The train from which he had alighted would not continue for another ten minutes. If Mlle. LeFevre were what Yates assumed her to be, she would not have followed on the next train, but would have taken an express east. And he had started west to help Carlos.

"Take my bags back to the Los Angeles express," he said to the waiting porter.

Five minutes later he was sitting in the dining car, unfolding the Albuquerque *Morning Herald*. Upon the front page, staring him in the face, was a photograph of King Carlos under a two-column headline in which he expressed his opinion of the royalists of Berania, his country in general, republican forms of government and so forth. Will read the lurid interview with increasing disgust.

How it was possible for a man as intelligent as the Secretary of State to read this statement and not realize that the person responsible for it was a rascal, was beyond his comprehension. And, what did the secretary mean by saying that he expressed the same sentiments which Carlos had expressed to Will?

Carlos said he abhorred civil war and that he admired the peaceful and prosperous manner in which America conducted herself, but he would be the last man in the world to sneer at his own country and express the hope that his loyal supporters be shot down by machine guns.

This interview was intended for consumption in Berania. Will had been correct in surmising that the republicans had set up the puppet in New York to create a bad impression of the character of the exiled king. The statement would.disgust thinking people in America and Europe with King Carlos, but it would not affect the royalist movement, at least in Will's opinion.

Knowing Carlos, the royalist leaders would assume it was a fake interview and, while the republicans would broadcast it, the royalists generally, those who could read and write, would consider it republican propaganda.

Its effect on Carlos would be appalling. It was likely to bring him out of his hiding place, cause him to issue a statement and thus supply his enemies with the information they were seeking. The quicker Will got to Los Angeles and restrained the ex-monarch the better for his welfare.

He still had twenty-four hours on the train and in that time Carlos would probably take some rash action. If he only knew where to reach him! If there were only something he could do! The inaction was galling him.

They were passing through the New Mexico desert. It was hot, dusty, disagreeable, and he was so nervous that he could not sleep. He was fed up with his drawing room and made his way to the club car. His wound did not pain him as much as it had yesterday. In a few days he would be perfectly well. He probably would need to be perfectly well.

IN THE CLUB car he was pounced upon by Goldsmith, the film producer, who held a newspaper in his hand and was smiling from ear to ear.

"Did you see the papers, Mr. Jervis?" he demanded. "What a man that king is. This will make him popular from coast to coast and build him into the biggest box office card in the business."

"I have no use for a bird that fouls his own nest," said Will sourly.

Goldsmith looked hurt.

"That's no way to talk about a friend," he protested. "What did Berania do for him? Kicked him out. We're a republican country ain't we? The people that buy tickets for pictures ain't got no use for kings. Well, here's a real live king that thinks just the way they do. He'd rather be nobody in the U.S.A. than a king in Europe. That's the way we like to hear kings talk. I tell you, the film will gross three millions and it won't be so terribly expensive to make."

"When do you start work?"

Goldsmith laughed. "That shows what you know about pictures. We've started. In a week already we spent a hundred thousand on big sets. We got newsreels from Madrova showing the fighting in the streets. We got the newsreel showing you and him getting out of the plane in Paris. I'm frank with you; that's why I need you in the picture. We already got you in some scenes and you might as well make money out of it."

"I've read nothing about the king signing a contract with you."

"They held up the statement till he gave the interview about the new outbreak in Berania. They will follow that up with the announcement in a couple of days that he has signed with me for fifteen thousand dollars a week."

"Do you mean to say he is being paid that much?"

"I don't say it; the papers say it. In confidence, we are paying him fifty thousand for the picture with an option at ten thousand a week. You got to say twice as much because they don't believe you anyway."

"And when does this King of Berania start for Los Angeles?"

"A week from to-day. Say, nothing like it has ever been known. He comes in a private car with 'King of Berania' painted on the sides of it. He has his own chef and his own bodyguard in green and gold uniforms. I'm arranging brass bands and receptions at every stop. Such a ballyhoo never was before."

"Marvelous," said Will, compelled to smile at the spectacle conjured up by the words of the showman.

"And when he hits L.A. the whole city will turn out. I'm trying to fix it to get the State militia to be in the parade, and we'll have two hundred police for a bodyguard."

"You do things in a big way," admired Will. "Do you know what happened to Mlle. LeFevre?"

"Reine de la Reine?" Goldsmith corrected. "Sure. The fool girl got all mussed up with the shooting on that station yesterday and missed the train. She wired me to take care of her luggage and said she would be along on the next train."

"Well," said Will, "I'm going to try to take a nap."

Goldsmith grasped his arm.

"Be reasonable," he pleaded. "I give you five thousand dollars to play a bit in this film. What do you say?"

"No."

"I lift it to seven thousand, five hundred."

"Not for what you are paying your king, Mr. Goldsmith."

"I introduce you to a lot of pretty girls," he said with a roguish leer.

Will shook his head firmly, rose and made his way back to his drawing room.

CHAPTER XVIII

A COUNCIL OF WAR

JERVIS HAD READ the dispatch in the Albuquerque newspaper containing the interview with the supposed dethroned King of Berania. The New York newspapers made very much more of it, and it was published verbatim that morning in London, Paris, Berlin and Madrova.

In the Beranian capital it caused a tremendous anti-royalist demonstration upon which the government gazed with a benevolent eye. Smaller demonstrations occurred in other cities, but there were counter anti-republican demonstrations which were only suppressed by profuse use of police and troops.

In the palace where King Carlos and his ancestors had reigned for centuries there was a conference of the four men who were the Republic of Berania. These were General Raquel Torres, a black-whiskered, hard-eyed martinet who was provisional president; Count Ramon Ysidro, secretary of the treasury; Señor Tomasso Martinez, secretary of state and Señor Antonio Muchardo, tribune of the people. They sat in the old council chamber and Torres occupied the chair in which Carlos had sat and which still bore, at the top of its high back, the gold crown.

And, just as Carlos had asked his prime minister a certain question, General Torres asked that question of the secretary of state.

"What is your opinion of the situation?"

"Very serious," replied Count Ysidro, who was a small, thin

dark man with a tiny mustache waxed at the ends. "They expect us to perform miracles in six months. It is my opinion that Carlos has only to land on our coast and the whole country will acclaim him. Burzio's army is gaining a thousand recruits an hour."

"But listen to the anti-Carlist demonstration outside," said the president.

"Artificial," stated the tribune of the people. "My agents report that the masses were absolutely indifferent, and if I had not had twenty-four hours' notice of the interview to work up enthusiasm there would have been none. There is none of the expected resentment of the wild life led in New York by Carlos despite the lurid accounts of it which our newspapers have not failed to publish."

"The fact is, Señor President," said the secretary of state, "that our government has not only disappointed the peasants, but the real republicans are bitterly hostile because we have not held a general election. They accuse you of being a dictator, not a president."

"A dictator," said Torres, "is exactly what this country needs."

YSIDRO grinned. "And exactly what it doesn't want. You are commander in chief. Can you still depend upon the army?"

"Until we lose a big battle," confessed Torres. "Most of our officers are royalists at heart. They were forced by their soldiers to declare for the republic and they will turn their coats when they think it is safe. The damn peasants are refusing to pay their taxes on the ground that they were promised that there would be no taxes under the republic. We can't shoot and jail them all. Our only hope is to smash this revolt rapidly. I'm taking the field in person just as soon as we have the news which will take the heart out of the royalists."

"But we can't expect that while this cursed Yankee, Jervis, is alive."

"They've missed him twice," said Torres, stroking his beard. "He can't escape us indefinitely."

"Well," said Ysidro flatly, "the interview upon which we counted so much went flat. And Burzio is not fool enough to let it be published in the province he controls. Even here in Madrova most of the people suspect we invented it. They know King Carlos pretty well, general."

"It has created a tremendous revulsion of feeling against him in Paris and London," declared the tribune of the people.

Torres shrugged his shoulders. "Unfortunately the state of mind of Paris and London is no help to us in Madrova. You say, count, that the American government is now fully convinced that Gomez is King Carlos?"

"Yes. The remarkable resemblance, the disappearance of Carlos and our production of the passport of Carl Decker have persuaded them."

The door of the council chamber opened suddenly and a person in the uniform of a colonel of the Republic of Berania entered in haste. He moved around the big table and proffered a long envelope to the president.

"From Sepoia, your excellency," he stated.

Torres tore it open while the others watched him with tense interest. He scowled as he read.

"Burzio sallied out of the town and fell upon the twentieth division with overwhelming numbers," he said crisply. "The division was cut to pieces, and Gama, its fool of a general, was killed. General Sanchez, in command of our forces, is retreating slowly and appealing for aid."

Count Ysidro expelled his breath noisily. "A victory! Exactly what Burzio needed. You'll have to move south with the strongest force you can collect, general."

"I'll send out my orders immediately, but I want the piece of news which will be worth a couple of army corps. Send the cable, count."

"With Jervis alive, it's too risky, sir."

Torres thumped the table. "I can't wait, you fool. Every hour is precious now. Tell them to account for Jervis as quickly as possible. You can ship the whole outfit to California immediately. Send that message."

"What is the message?" asked the tribune of the people.

Torres pushed back his chair and frowned upon him. "You'll know soon enough. It is a message which will cause this rebellion to melt into thin air."

"As tribune of the people," bleated Muchardo, "I have an excellent right to know—"

"And who appointed you tribune of the people?" roared the general. "You may be sure that I am acting in the best interests of the republic. This meeting is adjourned. I am moving south with fifty thousand men at seven o'clock to-morrow morning."

CHAPTER XIX

"PRO PATRIA"

THE MESSAGE OF which Torres had spoken reached New York at ten o'clock that night. It was delivered to the oily secretary of Alfonso Gomez as he and his chief arrived at their hotel from attendance at the theater. Both were in full evening dress and Gomez wore in his buttonhole the rosette of the Order of the Lion of Berania.

The hotel clerk took the cablegram from a pigeonhole and handed it to the secretary as the latter asked for the key of the suite occupied by Gomez and himself.

"Good evening, your majesty," said the clerk, beaming.

Gomez shook his head reproachfully. "Not majesty," he said in a tone which belied his words. "What's in the cablegram, Philip?" he asked in the Beranian tongue.

The secretary displayed it. His expression was suddenly glazed, but his chief was not looking at him.

"Pro patria," said Gomez. "Latin. What's the sense of sending nonsense like that?"

"It means that they approve of the interview you gave out yesterday."

"Well, why didn't they say, *"Viva?"* *"Pro patria!"* It's my opinion that Torres is losing his mind."

"Let us go upstairs," said the secretary. "The ladies will come at midnight."

"Ah, yes, the ladies," replied Gomez with eyes which grew

bright. "I wish to change my collar. It is so cursed hot in this city."

They entered their suite and the pretender threw himself into a chair.

"Twenty-five minutes of twelve. Time for a bottle of wine before the girls arrive."

He rose and flung off his dress coat, which he tossed upon a divan, and reseated himself. "The girls," he repeated. "My friend, I shall never cease to be grateful to you for searching me out. I was at my wit's end in Cannes. I had dropped my last *mille* note in the baccarat room and then you came and life became a dream of happiness. I have played my part well, eh?"

"Faultlessly," admitted the secretary. "My principals are delighted with your impersonation. Hence the cablegram."

"But such an idiotic message. *Pro patria,* I have no country. Even if my father was a king, my mother was an Italian peasant and I lived all my life in the South of France. What the devil do I care for Berania? *Pro patria!* That's part of a Latin quotation. I shall remember the rest of it in a moment."

He picked up a newspaper, turned to an editorial on his interview and began to read it. The secretary came up behind his chair and bent slightly to read over his shoulder.

"I have it!" exclaimed Gomez. "The whole quotation. *'Dulci et decorum est pro patria mori—' Ah!*" His voice broke off, he gasped, his eyes distended. For the secretary had grasped the top of his chair with his left hand, and had lifted on high a long glittering blade. It fell so swiftly that Gomez had no time to evade it. It penetrated inside his left shoulder blade and its point descended into the heart. He stiffened, moaned slightly, shivered, and was dead.

"It is sweet and proper to die for one's country," repeated the secretary, who was pale as chalk.

He stepped back, lifted his victim's head and let it fall again upon his breast. He drew a handkerchief from his pocket and wiped his brow, then carefully wiped the smooth ebony hilt of the stiletto which protruded from the back of the unfortunate masquerader.

He emitted a deep sigh. His eyes were filled with terror and he sat down to steady himself. Five long minutes passed and then he pulled himself together and picked up the telephone.

"**QUICK,** for God's sake!" he exclaimed. "King Carlos has been assassinated! I think he is dead!"

He hung up the instrument and began to pace the room. From the day he arrived in America with the half-brother of King Carlos, he had been aware of what, eventually, he might be commanded to do and he had laid his plans well, but there was always the chance that they would go awry.

A minute passed and running feet were heard in the corridor. A fist pounded on the door. He rose to answer it and almost fainted as a horrible thought crossed his mind. That fool Gomez—he had filled out the quotation of which *"Pro patria"* was a part. Might not some American detective do likewise and trace the connection between the message and the murder? Too late to destroy the cablegram!

He opened the door. There entered the hotel manager, a doctor, the big red-faced house detective and Briggs, the secret service man.

The secretary pointed dramatically to the figure doubled over in the big chair.

"His majesty," he said brokenly. "Murdered."

The detective crossed to the dead man and took in the situation in a glance, "Stabbed from behind with a stiletto," he said. "Don't anybody touch it. He's dead as a haddock."

"How did this happen?" demanded the hotel manager.

The secretary plunged into his carefully prepared story.

"I don't know," he declared. "We entered our suite. His majesty—this is no time for incognito—King Carlos seated himself and picked up the evening paper. He commanded me to fetch him a clean collar. I went into the bedroom. I do not think I was out of this room a couple of minutes. I returned with the collar and saw him as you see him. I rushed to him. I saw the knife. I telephoned for assistance. That is all."

"I saw you come in," said the house detective. "Not more than ten minutes ago."

"I trailed you here from the theater," said the secret service man. "I saw you take the elevator. I thought you might be going out again—"

"We were," the secretary replied. "Two ladies were to call for us and we were going to a night club."

"What's your idea of what happened?" demanded the house detective.

"I can only conclude, sir, that there was a man concealed in the room, perhaps behind those heavy draperies and, when I left the room, he rushed upon the king, struck, and ran out of the apartment, down the corridor and left by the stairs or the elevator."

"Why should anybody want to kill him? Has he been robbed?"

"I don't think there was time for it."

The doctor who had been examining the body now reported.

"His watch and wallet are on him," he stated.

"Did you hear any sound, the opening and closing of a door?" asked the house detective.

"No, sir."

Briggs took up the questioning.

"You were only out of the room a couple of minutes. There was time to head off the assassin if you had rushed to the door and into the corridor. You might at least have got a look at him."

"Sir, I was overcome by horror. I was petrified for a moment. I could not understand that my royal master had been murdered in the moment or two in which I had left him alone. As soon as I recovered myself, after a minute or two, perhaps, I rushed to the telephone. What more could I do?"

"You speak of him as your royal master," said the hotel manager who was trembling at the thought of the damage the murder of a king would cause to his establishment. "You have always insisted that he was not King Carlos."

"My friend," said the secretary, "that was necessary because we entered America illegally. We did not wish to embarrass the government of the United States. Since he is dead there is no longer necessity for pretense. You are looking upon the body of King Carlos of Berania."

"That's right," said Briggs. "I've known it all along. He was the king, all right."

THE HOTEL man sighed. "Then there is no possibility of this lamentable affair being kept quiet. It will ruin the hotel, and our patronage is—"

"I'll call up police headquarters," the house detective said as he picked up the phone. "We've got one clew, the dagger."

"Mr. Dalmoro," said Briggs to the secretary, "have you any idea why he was killed?"

The secretary nodded lugubriously. "The reason is evident to me," he replied. "His majesty was very headstrong. He would listen to me only up to a certain point. I pleaded with him not to make that statement to the newspapers yesterday."

"Sounded like a good statement to me," Briggs asserted. "The Beranian government couldn't take any exceptions to that."

"The government, no, but do you realize that it must have infuriated the royalists?

"No doubt there have filtered into New York many Beranians exiled by their royalist sentiments whose only hope of recovering their estates was the restoration of the king. They expected that he would return to his country and head the revolt against the republic. When he expressed himself as contented with the republic, they considered him a traitor and a recreant. It is possible that he was killed by these fanatics and that the motive was revenge."

Briggs nodded sagely, and the others seemed impressed. The

house detective, after talking with police headquarters, laid down the phone.

"Guess he was killed by one of his own countrymen, all right," he observed. "That's a foreign knife. The head of the homicide squad will be right over."

As he finished speaking the telephone rang and the detective answered it.

"Miss DeLancy and Miss DeVere calling on Mr, Gomez," said the operator.

Covering the mouthpiece with his hand the detective turned to the secretary.

"Couple of dames downstairs. What'll I tell them?"

"Nothing," cried the manager. "They are show girls. They'll inform the newspapers immediately."

"What of it?" asked the detective. "The papers will have it anyway. Can't keep this out."

"Please inform them," requested the secretary, "that Mr. Gomez is ill and cannot keep the engagement."

"That'll do it."

He dismissed the young women and laid down the phone.

"May I remind you that nothing has been done to apprehend the miscreant?" remarked the secretary.

"He was out of the hotel before we reached this room," replied the house man. "You had the chance to spot him and you missed it. How long had you been with his majesty, mister?"

"Many years."

"But you were not with him when he left Madrova."

"No. He was accompanied only by the American, Jervis. I joined him in Paris by prearrangement."

"It's tough on you," said the detective sympathetically. "Did you know that there's a drop of blood on your shirt front?".

"Very likely. I rushed to his majesty, unaware that he had been stabbed. I bent over him and then I discovered the knife."

He drew forth his handkerchief and wiped his eyes.

The phone rang again.

"Lieutenant Hoffman of the homicide squad is on his way up," stated the operator.

CHAPTER XX

TRUTH CRUSHED TO EARTH

THE ASSASSINATION OF the ex-king of Berania in a suite in a New York hotel created a tremendous sensation throughout Europe and the United States. It caused consternation in Washington, utter dismay in Sepoia and jubilation in government circles in Madrova, capital of Berania.

The Duke of Burzio, Carlos's supporter, endeavored at first to persuade his followers that it was only a canard invented by the republicans to offset the effect of the rebel victory, but he himself was convinced later in the day when an official dispatch from Washington confirmed the report that it was King Carlos who was dead.

The dethroned monarch of Berania, according to the official report, had entered the United States upon an American passport issued to one Carl Decker.

It having been reported to Washington that a person resembling Carlos Aronhof was in New York City, appearing in public places, permitting it to be surmised that he was the exiled king whose disappearance from Paris had been puzzling Europe, an investigation was set afoot and it was established beyond a doubt that this individual, now calling himself Alfonso Gomez, was actually the ex-king.

As he had entered illegally, the State Department had been in conference with the immigration authorities with the intention of tactfully persuading him to leave the United States. It was a difficult situation in view of the exalted position he had

139

so recently occupied, and it was hoped that he would depart voluntarily. Unfortunately he fell a victim to an assassin before the United States government had been given a chance to move.

This was enough for the Duke of Burzio, who ordered that his army disband and the royal standard be furled, then entered one of his army airplanes and followed the route to Paris taken some months previous by King Carlos and Will Jervis.

The victorious royalist army scattered like chaff. It had been fighting for the king, and the king was dead, with no member of the royal line alive to replace him. It no longer had a cause.

WILL JERVIS alighted from the transcontinental express at 8.30 A.M. and encountered a newsboy, shouting the sensation, as he left the railroad station. He grasped a newspaper and, profoundly bewildered, read the lurid tale wired from New York.

It ran under an eight-column headline and was illustrated by a dozen pictures of the ex-king in various uniforms, all taken from the newspaper's morgue, or obituary cabinet. And he was confronted by a photograph of himself as the man who had rescued King Carlos in vain.

His porter waited impatiently and finally touched him on the arm.

"Your cab is here, sir," he said.

In a fog, Will followed him and got into the cab. During the journey to the Hotel Ambassador he continued to peruse the story. The thing seemed totally incomprehensible.

From the beginning he had been convinced that Alfonso Gomez was a creature of the government of Berania. Madrova had instructed him to strut about in New York. Madrova had ordered him to give out that contemptible interview. Madrova had made two attempts to assassinate Will Jervis because he was the only man in America who could denounce the impostor.

The republicans' purpose in setting up a false Aronhof in New York had not been clear to Jervis, but why go to such

Carl, in chauffeur's uniform, entered with a policeman.

trouble and expense if they intended to murder the impostor? And if Gomez had not been killed by Beranian agents, who had killed him?

According to the paper, the Secretary stated that he thought the murderer had been a royalist fanatic who disapproved of Carlos's cold-blooded refusal to sympathize with those in Berania who had raised the royal standard. That was possible.

Will was not aware that the cab had reached the Ambassador until the chauffeur spoke to him impatiently and the hotel porter waited expectantly.

He registered mechanically, received several letters and a telegram which he slipped into his pocket without glancing at, and he was ascending in the elevator when the fog suddenly cleared.

"By Jove!" he exclaimed.

"What did you say, sir?" asked the elevator boy.

"Nothing. No consequence."

The plot was now as clear as crystal. Its ingenuity was diabolical. Only men totally without conscience would be able to conceive and execute such an abominable crime.

Thanks to Will's assistance, the real king had evaded his enemies and they had lost track of him completely for months. While Carlos lived, the new government would be sitting upon a powder magazine. Gomez, a man who resembled him like a brother—who, most likely, was an illegitimate brother of whose existence King Carlos was unaware—had been shipped to New York and publicly displayed.

The original object was to draw the real Carlos from cover. Upon the very first night of the masquerade the pretender had been unlucky enough to encounter Will Jervis, who failed to be deceived. Immediately the gang around the pretender undertook to remove Jervis from the land of the living, and almost succeeded.

King Carlos, however, did not bob up as they had expected, but they learned by tampering with Jervis's mail that he was somewhere in Southern California and agents were immediately dispatched to Los Angeles to eliminate him. When Jervis, also, started for California, the Beranians were on the job. Evidently their plans did not require him to lead them to Carl's hiding place. From the king's letter they were aware that Jervis was no better informed than they. They wanted Jervis dead where he could tell no tales.

When they had murdered Carlos Aronhof, the actor in New York would immediately vanish and then the body of the real king would be discovered and it would be presumed that it was that of the man who had been showing himself in New York.

But a serious royalist rising had taken place in Berania and the government was probably in greater danger than it permitted the world to believe. That explained the interview given out by Gomez which was expected to discourage the royalists. It seemed to have failed and the Duke of Burzio had fallen upon a government force and annihilated it.

To a government already unpopular, a single military defeat

was apt to be fatal, but one thing could save it—the death of the king. They had no time to wait for the Aronhof to be unearthed. They had succeeded in convincing Washington that the man in New York was the veritable Aronhof. So, they would kill him and risk a subsequent exposure.

That was it. His own people had murdered the poor wretch who had been posing as a king for several weeks.

THE WHOLE thing flashed through Will's mind as he walked toward his room. It was probably the first time in history that it was possible to kill a king and end a royal line. There wasn't anybody living with the slightest claim to the throne of Berania and the rebellion would pop like an exploded balloon.

Now all Berania had to do was to mop up and he, Will Jervis, was the object of the mopping. With Jervis out of the way, King Carlos could come out from retirement and shout himself hoarse if he liked. He would be greeted with derision. Most likely the government of Berania would produce evidence that he was a person named Alfonso Gomez, related perhaps to the Aronhofs by the left hand. But it was necessary to kill Jervis.

Will smiled grimly as he considered that phase of the situation. Twice he had narrowly escaped assassination and Yates had pointed out to him that Los Angeles, because of its closeness to the Mexican border, was likely to be the focal point of a cloud of Beranian assassins posing as Mexicans.

Well, before he died, he would throw a monkey wrench into the machinery. He put in a call for Assistant Secretary of State Downes at Washington. In half an hour the connection was made.

"Jervis calling," he said.

"Hello, Will," replied the assistant secretary. "You've heard the news?"

"The man who was killed in New York was not King Carlos."

"You haven't seen our statement, I suppose."

"No."

"As far as we are concerned, he *is* King Carlos. It has let me out of a predicament. I was a fool to listen to you and the Ambassador. His death has enabled me to wiggle out of it. He has been positively identified by a score of people in New York who knew him."

"Who had a glimpse of him, perhaps, in Madrova."

"He has the passport you know about. His secretary admits he is the king. The case is closed."

"I'm going to reopen it."

"You're one against a score."

"I'll fly to New York."

"He will be cremated first thing in the morning," said the secretary. "The fur is flying round here because he was illegally admitted. Of course we claim we just found it out and were about to deport him."

"I'll produce the real Carlos."

"Where is he?"

"Out here. I don't know just where."

"Look here, old man. This ought to be just what he wants, if you are not mistaken, as I am certain you are. He doesn't have to worry about assassins any more. He'll probably be tickled to death. Anyway, we're all washed up with him. Good-by."

Will hung up in wild anger. It was exactly what might be expected of a politician whose good nature had persuaded him to wink at a law violation and who was now frightened and determined to cover up. Well, he'd find Carlos and together they would expose this outrage—if the Beranian assassins didn't get in their work first.

CHAPTER XXI

JAIL DOORS OPEN

WILL ORDERED BREAKFAST and, as he sat down, realized that there was a bulge in his pocket. He dragged forth his mail and observed, for the first time, a telegram. He opened it and exclaimed with astonishment, dismay and satisfaction. Astonishment because it was from Carlos, dismay because the king was in jail, and satisfaction because he could get in touch with him immediately.

Without waiting to eat his breakfast, he rushed down stairs—the enforced rest during the journey across the continent had been very beneficial to his wounded leg—secured a cab and was driven to police headquarters.

"I want to see a man named Carl Decker," he demanded at the office.

"Name and address, please," replied the attendant.

He gave them. "What's the charge against him?"

"Held on suspicion and for questioning by the Federal authorities."

"Can I see him?"

"You'll have to talk to Captain Adams first. This case is in his hands."

"I'll be glad to."

Will was conducted into the presence of the cheerful but efficient police official who had questioned Carl.

"You got here quick," said the captain suspiciously. "The telegram only went off to New York yesterday morning."

"I was on my way to Los Angeles, captain. It was readdressed and I found it at the Hotel Ambassador this morning. Kindly tell me the charge against Mr. Decker."

"Well, it's like this, Mr. Jervis." He paused. "Is this man a friend of yours?"

"He is."

"We happened to pick up this chauffeur with fifty thousand dollars' worth of stolen jewels on him."

"Chauffeur! Do you mean to say Carl is a chauffeur?"

"Yep. Working for Mrs. Mason Swasey in Beverly Hills."

"Beverly Hills. That's out of your jurisdiction, isn't it?"

"All I know is that a couple of men brought him into this office," said the captain, slightly confused. "Now it stands to reason that no chauffeur would have a fortune in jewels unless he stole them."

"This one has," replied Will quickly. "It seems that no charge of theft is preferred against him."

"We expect to find the owner in a few hours now."

"You won't. The gems are the property of Mr. Decker. I can vouch for that."

"Yeah? And who's going to vouch for you?"

Will laughed. "Would the President of the United States satisfy you?"

"He certainly would."

"Well, he knows me. And the Governor of California, whom I entertained when I was secretary of the American Legation in Berania."

The captain laughed genially. "I know you're all right, Mr. Jervis. You're the fellow that flew away with the King of Berania. Didn't do the poor guy much good. They killed him in New York last night."

"I read the newspaper account. Will you kindly release Mr. Decker at once?"

"Well, now, I can't do that. How does he happen to have these sparklers?"

"Mr. Decker is a man who was formerly rich. He comes of an old European family. These are family jewels. I can understand his plight."

"I can't," said the captain, grinning. "You be responsible for his appearance if it turns out you're—ahem—mistaken?"

"Certainly."

"Well, that's all right, but we were going to notify the immigration people. He's a foreigner who admits he's only been in the country six months and he admits he has no passport."

"If you haven't notified the immigration people, can't you forget it?"

"No. I'll tell you, Mr. Jervis. There is a person in this town with a heck of a lot of influence who has it in for this fellow. If the theft charge is dropped, he'll insist upon the illegal entry."

JERVIS sighed. "Will you kindly put in a long distance call for Assistant Secretary of State Downes, in Washington?"

"Sure, if you'll pay for it."

"I'll do that."

In twenty minutes Downes was on the phone again.

"Jervis speaking."

"You're getting to be a pest," said the Assistant Secretary irascibly.

"A certain person has been picked up by the Los Angeles police because he has lost his passport. Carl Decker is his name."

"Oh, Lord, you've found him!" exclaimed the Secretary with a heavy sigh.

"I am talking from police headquarters. Will you kindly tell Captain Adams that you know this man and that he is all right and should be released immediately?"

"I suppose I'll have to," the Secretary said resignedly. "Put him on."

Considerably puffed up at a personal conversation with a

high government official, Captain Adams took the phone. He listened.

"Certainly, sir. A word from you is good enough for me. I'll have Decker turned loose right away."

He rang off and called the jail office. "Please send the man booked as Carl Decker right down to my office. Give him back his stuff. He's sprung."

He grinned at Jervis. "You seem to have a drag in high places."

"You'd be surprised," replied Will with twinkling eyes.

Five minutes later a young man in chauffeur's livery entered the room, accompanied by a policeman. He stood there calmly for an instant, then saw Jervis. His fine face lighted and he rushed toward Will with outstretched hand.

"My friend!" he exclaimed. "Did you come to my aid by air express?"

"I was on my way, and your telegram was sent after me. I regret exceedingly your unpleasant experience—" He was about to add "sir," but choked it off.

"Oh, it might have been worse," said the king lightly. "I slept very well, as a matter of fact."

The police captain was staring at him in astonishment. "Say," he declared, "I suppose it's seeing you with Mr. Jervis, but if I didn't know he was dead I'd think you was the King of Berania with his mustache shaved off."

"But you happen to know that he is dead," said Will, with a warning glance at the astonished Decker.

"Well, it seems it was all a mistake, Decker," said the captain. "You owned these jewels all the time. I'll have 'em for you in a jiffy."

The king frowned at him. "The sooner the better. I shall not soon forget this treatment."

"Say, we treated you pretty good. You ought to see the way we treat real crooks," replied the captain, not in the least perturbed. "Here you are, feller. Check 'em and make sure they are all there."

CARL obeyed and nodded in satisfaction. He disposed of the gems in different pockets.

"Listen," said Captain Adams. "With all these Chicago gunmen in town, you'll be murdered in about ten minutes if they find what you carry on your person. Better put those in a safe."

"And very good advice, too," Will remarked. "Come along, Mr. Decker. Have you breakfasted?"

"A cup of very bad coffee, that's all."

"Well, I'll tell you everything while we breakfast. And as soon as a bank is open we must put your gems in safety."

"What did he mean by saying I was dead?" asked Carl as they left police headquarters.

"The man in New York was assassinated last night."

Carl looked startled and then said: "Poor fool! The fate that was intended for me."

"I'm not so sure. Does your majesty mind going into this little cafeteria?"

The king laughed like a boy. "My very dear friend, I mind nothing. For ten days I ate with servants and I have just come from a common jail."

"I grieve that you have been reduced to such straits, sir."

Carl slapped him on the shoulder jovially. "Don't be so respectful," he commanded. "I'm a plain American. For months I've been elbowed and shoved by your not very polite countrymen. I have been working for a vulgar old woman and touching my hat to her bounder of a son. I've been subjected to familiarities from butlers, servant wenches and fellow chauffeurs. I rather like it, Will."

"If I had only known—"

"I stand on my own feet, my friend. Like a fool, I hoarded these baubles and became a servant rather than sell one of them. Do you know what I'm going to do? I'm going to sell them all. No more king business for me. I'm going to live and die an obscure person. How long must I wait to become a full-fledged American citizen?"

"Five years. Now, I'm going to begin at the beginning and tell you what has happened and what I surmise. First, let's get a tray and pick out our dishes."

"I am familiar with the procedure in cafeterias," Carl assured him.

THEY seated themselves, and Will began his tale, to which the king listened with rising interest and indignation. He had not read the newspapers for several days, and he was unaware of the shameful interview given out by the false Carlos. Nor was he aware of the victory gained by the Duke of Burzio. His reaction, however, to the existing situation was not what Will had expected.

"If the revolt had made headway," he said thoughtfully, "I would be compelled, out of regard for my adherents, to go back and take the field with them. While I refused responsibility for a civil war, in a battle between my friends and foes I would be unable to remain neutral. But the assassination has removed that necessity. By this time the royalist army will have disbanded and the alleged republic will be more firmly established than ever. I no longer desire to sit on a throne. I am content. I wish to live tranquilly in California."

Their eyes met, and the king, for no reason, blushed furiously.

"Ah," said Jervis softly, "you've met a girl. You are in love."

"Correct," Carl admitted. "I am in love with a very marvelous young woman."

Will arched his eyebrows. "The daughter of your employer, eh?"

"No," Carl replied, smiling. "Not at all. A very poor girl, a working girl."

"You'll quickly get tired of that sort."

"Never. And if she marries me, it will be for life. I have no intention of being dragged back to a throne and forced to divorce the woman I love because she is a commoner."

"A very pretty idyl," said Will shrewdly. "And does she know who she is marrying?"

"That is the marvelous part of it. She thinks I am a chauffeur. She thinks, however, that I can do better than that. She loves me for myself alone—that is to say, I think she loves me."

"My dear sir, you don't seem to realize that you are in no position to marry and settle down. The royalists may believe that you are dead, but General Torres and his gang know better. While you live, they will consider you a menace and they won't rest until they remove you. Incidentally, until they eliminate me."

"My great regret is that you are involved in my unfortunate affairs,"

"Don't worry about me. We've got to consider your safety."

"What can I do?" demanded the king. "You and I know I am alive and the little coterie in Madrova know it, but your government and the rest of the world believe me dead. There have always been pretenders arising to claim the throne of a monarch supposed to be dead, but they have never succeeded. If I deny this accusation, I shall not be believed."

"With me to identify you?"

"Even with you. Two men against the world. Furthermore, we inform them where I am to be found, which is something to be avoided."

"They know where I am to be found. They've trailed me and attempted my life *en route.* We must separate, your majesty. Let me know your address and don't try to communicate with me. I'll call you, when necessary, on the telephone."

"I want you to meet Dalma Dawning."

Will almost laughed at the preposterous name. "A stage name, no doubt," he said in extenuation.

"I do not know. I have only known her two or three days. It

was love at first sight. Being in love, my friend, is better than being a king."

Will sighed. "If you are sure the object is worthy," he said, thinking of Mlle. LeFevre.

"Well, there is a little hotel in a district called Sherman. It is the Fanwick. I shall get a room there and await news of you. I wish you to meet Dalma as soon as possible."

"It will be a pleasure. Your majesty—"

"Will, I insist that you call me Carl," said the king with his winning smile.

"Carl, then. I was too young to get into the World War, but I come of a family of fighting men. It is pretty evident that the masses of your people want you back. This assassination in New York was a desperate stroke. Burzio apparently was carrying all before him. The murderers in Madrova will get a respite from the report of your death. No doubt this rebellion will collapse immediately. It was a break for Torres that our government officially confirmed the death of King Carlos. However, I have no desire to be a target for marksmen for the rest of my life and you have but little chance of escaping them for any great length of time. For the sake of my own skin, I'm afraid I've got to put you back on the throne of Berania."

CARLOS laughed loudly and cast a whimsical glance around the dingy cafeteria in a sordid corner of the city of Los Angeles, eight thousand miles away from the pomp and circumstance of the royal establishment of Madrova.

"Not interested, my friend," he said. "I'm in love with a little American picture actress. Imagine the reception she would get in Madrova if I presented her as my queen."

"You'll have to forget the love business," said Jervis gravely. "If you marry that girl, she'll be a widow in a month or a year. You don't want to do that to her. And, as you say, you can't very well make her Queen of Berania and you don't want to make her the victim of a morganatic marriage."

"No king of Berania can marry a woman not of royal blood, according to an ancient law. So I shall not return to Berania."

"Now look here, the common people had nothing to do with your overthrow. Most likely they didn't hear that you had abdicated until six months after you had left, and then they got down their old fowling pieces and joined Burzio's army. You can't let them down, Carl. And we can't allow those criminals in Madrova to go unpunished."

"All very well," the king said, "but how are we going to punish them? You have a plan, of course."

"Well, not exactly," the American admitted, "but I'll have one. I can force our government to admit it was mistaken in identifying Gomez as King Carlos and can secure your official recognition as the real Aronhof when the time is ripe. There are at least a thousand people in Madrova whom you can convince of your identity when you appear there. That's going to be all right. But we've got to wait tor the right moment and, in the meantime, remain alive. We'll go to the Security Trust Company, up the street a bit, and deposit your gewgaws and then we'll separate."

"Very good."

"Will you promise me not to propose to that girl? You have no right."

Carl nodded gloomily. "That is true. I give you my word. But only until you tell me your plan."

"What are you going to do now?"

"Return to Beverly Hills, get my belongings from the garage of Madam Swasey and move into the hotel I spoke of."

"Be very careful to cover your tracks. You may be watched."

After securing a safety deposit box in the name of Carl Decker, the friends separated and Will took a taxi back to his hotel. Despite his bold words to King Carlos, he was fully cognizant of the immensity of the job he proposed to undertake and, as yet, without a notion of how to accomplish it.

He had to overthrow the government of a nation of twelve

million people on the other side of the Atlantic and do it before
one of the hired assassins of that government put an end to his
own life and that of Carlos.

CHAPTER XXII

WILL'S DARING PLAN

WILL HAD NOT boasted when he declared that he could make the American government admit error in its identification of Alfonso Gomez as Carlos Aronhof. Downes, after all, was an honorable man. In a real emergency, he would resign his office and admit publicly that he had permitted the entry of King Carlos on the passport of Carl Decker. Will had no desire to place him in such an embarrassing position, but he would do it if it became necessary.

In the privacy of his chamber, he drew the automatic which he had taken from the person of Señor Grandez and made sure that it was in good order. At any moment the enemy might strike and fortune might not be good to him next time.

At one o'clock he descended to the main dining room for lunch and was being conducted to a table when a voice which he could not mistake called softly.

"M. Jervis."

Seated alone at a table to his left was Mlle. LeFevre, as vivid and enchanting as she had appeared at their first meeting.

"*Mademoiselle,* this is a surprise!" he exclaimed.

"Is it not? If you are alone, why not lunch with me?"

"I'd be delighted," he assured her truthfully. The sight of her banished momentarily from his mind the suspicions which her conduct and the suggestions of Yates had provoked.

"Was it not stupid of me," she demanded, "to miss the train and be left in a horrible spot in your New Mexico?"

"It was most distressing to me. I had looked forward to your company during the remainder of the journey. When did you arrive?"

"An hour ago."

"I cannot understand how it happened."

"Very simple. An Indian woman in the station was selling me the most beautiful rug. I heard shooting outside and I ran out to see what had happened. I saw a man lying dead and another man firing at an automobile which was driving away. Everything was such confusion and finally the conductor cried, 'All aboard.' I was about to get on the train when the Indian woman with a policeman stopped me and I found I was under arrest. It seems that I had the rug in my hand when I ran out of the station and the stupid woman thought I had stolen it. While I argued with them the train departed and I was left in that awful place."

As she told it the story seemed perfectly plausible to Will and he beamed upon her happily. And then he became aware of a faint elusive perfume, one not to be mistaken. It was "Heart of Cupid" which Yates was certain had been worn by the woman who rifled his luggage.

"Imagine me, *monsieur*," she continued. "I 'ave not even a nightdress, nothing but my little handbag in which, fortunately, was my money. Four hours I waited for the next train and it was not a de luxe train like that from which I had descended. But, *chut*, it is over! I am in this wonderful Los Angeles. And I am pleased to see you again."

"Are you going to remain in this hotel?"

"Perhaps. It is very expensive, but the studio pays my expenses. Am I not fortunate?"

JERVIS nodded. "Speaking of the studio, Mr. Goldsmith has lost his great box office attraction, according to the morning newspapers."

She clasped her hands excitedly.

"Horrible, was it not? Poor King Carlos! He was so young

and so handsome, and his death, it was so horrible. This is a lawless country, it appears, *monsieur.*"

He bridled. "Kings have been assassinated in Europe, I believe, when surrounded by their courtiers and their armies."

"Of course that is true. And no doubt it was one of his own countrymen who stabbed Carlos."

"No doubt. It makes the republic secure. As a Beranian you will be glad of that."

"But I am not a Beranian," she said with wide eyes. "How 'ave you thought that?"

"I beg your pardon. You are French. I forgot."

"You do not remember me very well, I fear," she said reproachfully.

"You are a person it is impossible to forget, whatever your nationality. Did you learn what the shooting was about?"

"Ah, yes. A miscreant attempted to kill a gentleman on our train by shooting at him through a car window and he was shot down by a government detective, so I was informed."

"Would you be surprised to learn that I was the person whose murder was attempted?"

She looked so genuinely shocked that she was either a marvelous actress or actually astonished and alarmed.

"You, M. Jervis? But who could wish to kill you?"

He shook his head. "I am sure I don't know. By the way, that perfume you wear; it's most unusual."

"I am so glad you 'ave escaped. It is a very nice perfume, but well known in Paris. It's named Cœur d'Eros."

"I don't suppose many people wear it in this country."

"Au contraire. It is on sale in all perfume shops. I have observed it upon so many American ladies that I consider giving it up. How absurd to discuss perfumes when you have just escaped death, *monsieur.*"

"Look!" he cried. "Goldsmith!"

The film producer had entered the dining room. His appearance, since Will had chatted with him on the train the day before, had changed astonishingly. His clothes hung on him as though he had lost twenty pounds overnight, which, of course, was impossible. There were huge black shadows under his eyes, his mouth seemed to have withdrawn so that the tip of his nose almost touched his chin, and he exuded an atmosphere of intense gloom.

He was passing by without seeing them when Mlle. LeFevre called to him. He started violently, looked displeased and then his eye rested upon Jervis. Here was one who would share his woe.

"How are you?" he asked. "Ain't this the most horrible thing that ever happened? What kind of a government have we got that it can't protect a man's investments?"

"What a dreadful way to regard a tragedy!" the young woman exclaimed.

Goldsmith scowled at her. "So you got here, eh? You might just as well turn around and go back to Paris. For you, I make a rotten program picture. Millions I lose because this king lets himself get stabbed in the heart."

Mlle. LeFevre stiffened and her fine eyes flashed.

"Fortunately I have finished my lunch," she said angrily. *"Au revoir,* M. Goldsmith." Despite Will's protests she left.

"BELIEVE it or not, that king film would have grossed four millions," said Goldsmith, indifferent to her departure. "Fifty thousand cash in advance I laid down for the contract and then the king up and died on me."

"Of course you will abandon the picture," Will hazarded.

"How can I?" Goldsmith wailed. "I signed a contract with the United Exhibitors to deliver it in four months or forfeit a quarter of a million. I got contracts from them grossing a million and a half for it and that's only the beginning. Just because this Carlos died, do you think them crooks will let me off the forfeit? Besides, I'm in a hundred thousand on the film out here already."

"Then all you have to do is put an actor in the rôle."

"I agreed to deliver the King of Berania."

"But you told me yourself you couldn't bill him as the king."

"Sure, but they knew he was. They were going to put on a whispering campaign."

"Then you must drop the picture?"

"What I got to do," said Goldsmith, "is to start work on it. The day I drop it, they take my quarter of a million out of escrow. In three months, I deliver it and then they refuse to accept it, but they got to sue me because it doesn't say in the contract that the hero is the King of Berania. It's a verbal agreement, that part of it."

"A question of veracity between you and another man?"

"Between me and seven other men," said Goldsmith sadly. "I can't get away with it."

Will clapped his hands together. "Never mind your lunch," he said. "You're not hungry. Come up to my room. I've got something to tell you which may give you an appetite."

"Nobody can ever give me an appetite again," Goldsmith declared solemnly, but he rose docilely and accompanied Will to the privacy of his chamber.

"Sit down," commanded Jervis. "You know that I am the friend of the King of Berania. I got him out of Madrova."

"What of it? Sure I know it. Didn't I offer you a contract? That's out. You wouldn't be any good to me now."

Will laughed. "Goldsmith," he said, "you've been swindled. You never had a contract with King Carlos."

"You're nuts. Right here I got it."

"You had a contract with Alfonso Gomez. He wasn't the king."

"Eh? Of course he was."

"A faker, Mr. Goldsmith. King Carlos is alive and here in Los Angeles. I left him an hour ago. It was to meet him that I came out here."

The producer stared at him, unbelieving.

"**I SAW** this impostor in New York," continued Will. "Fearing that I would betray him, he tried to have me assassinated in my apartment. You know an attempt was made to kill me upon the Transcontinental Express. Beranian agents, Mr. Goldsmith. They had to get rid of me to carry on their masquerade."

"A faker?" murmured the producer. "I gave fifty thousand to a faker? Oh, my God! What did they kill him for?"

"That I don't know. If you could make your picture with the real King Carlos—"

"But nobody would believe it was him. The government says he is dead."

"I guarantee to make the government change its mind."

"If you could prove he was the real thing—"

"I can swear to it. You can bring a score of people from Europe who know him well."

"But will he do it?" asked Goldsmith eagerly.

Will nodded. "Under certain conditions. As I understand it, you are going on with the picture anyway and your exhibitors cannot jump you until it is delivered and proves not to be as represented."

"That's right. I got three months' grace, though I bet they're spending my money, in their minds, right now."

"You will give out that you have found an actor who will play the part. You will make the picture with great secrecy—"

"That's the way we make all our pictures."

"Is there any way in which you could house the king and myself inside your studio walls during the time it takes to make this film?"

"Sure. I got a six-room Italian villa on the lot that I had to build five years ago for Jane Morton to get her to sign a new contract. Then sound came in, and she was terrible, and I had to buy up her contract. It's full of swell furniture."

"King Carlos is in hourly danger of assassination. Madrova knows perfectly well that the man in New York was an impostor and that the king is in. California. You don't want him killed when your picture is only half finished."

Goldsmith laughed. "They're not going to kill two kings on me. Say, I'll have him guarded like nobody's business."

"He'll make the film without charge, and I'll work in it without salary—"

The producer's eyes gleamed, but he made a polite protest.

"On this condition," Will went on. "You will throw away your scenario. I don't know what it is, but you'll be supplied with a much better story by me, a marvelous story, Mr. Goldsmith—"

"That's what you think, maybe—"

"And when you release the picture you will be authorized to announce that it was made by ex-King Carlos of Berania in person, and there will be no necessity of conducting a whispering campaign."

Goldsmith slapped his knee. "If I can do that, I don't care how rotten the story is. Mr. Jervis, I guess you've saved my life."

"How do you propose to guard his majesty?"

"Say, we got a system, now, that's almost perfect. Nobody ever sets foot on our lot unless we know all about them, and nobody on the pay roll knows anything about any picture they are not working on."

"I don't want Mlle. LeFevre admitted to the lot until this picture is finished."

Goldsmith looked amazed. "Say, I kind of thought you was stuck on her," he declared.

"My personal feelings have nothing to do with this. She is a Frenchwoman who has lived in Berania and knows the king by sight."

"Ah!"

"Can you arrange that all scenes in which he appears with the principals are without other witnesses, and that big scenes in which he appears will be saved to the very end?"

"I can't hold up all the big scenes, but I'll stick in some other fellow in his uniform and use long shots of him. We never let anybody look at plot shots. The way things are now, you got to watch for spies from other studios all the time."

"Very good," said Will. "King Carlos and I will move into that furnished house this afternoon."

GOLDSMITH drew a long breath and his eyes were glittering. His showman's imagination was already visualizing his triumph.

"There's only one thing," he said. "What in hell are you doing it for? I mean what do you and the king get out of it?"

"All that need interest you is that we are giving you a picture which will gross millions and are not charging you a cent."

"You swear on oath that you ain't ringing in a faker on me?"

"I am giving you for your leading man the real King Carlos of Berania."

Goldsmith nodded vehemently.

"And that's good enough for me," he declared. "No matter how rotten your story is, we can make it good."

"You can dramatize it as you like, but you cannot change the plot of this story. I must approve all sequences. As we have no contracts, we can walk out on you if we don't approve of what you're doing."

"I'd rather give you both big salaries and contracts."

"No doubt. You'll have to do business on my terms."

"You got me."

"How were you so rash as to risk $250,000 cash on a film which depended entirely upon the life of one man? Suppose he had died a natural death during the making of your picture?"

Goldsmith shrugged his big shoulders. "If you ain't a gambler you ain't got no business in the film business. I figured he couldn't drink himself to death in only three months. I took the chance."

"Well, if any rumor gets out that it is King Carlos who is making this photoplay, whether or not it is your fault—"

"I'm saying nothing."

"You might think it is wise to tip off these exhibitors to keep them from instituting legal action against you—"

"They can't get that money out of escrow for three months. I'll tell those lowlifes nothing."

"I'll give you the plot of this story to-morrow. I can promise you it will be sensational beyond your wildest expectations."

"The wilder the better," the producer said, grinning. "Mr. Jervis, do you mind if I kiss you?"

"I certainly do."

"I'll have my own cook and valet installed in the cottage when you get there. Say, I'm a happy man."

"Good luck to you."

When the producer had departed Will went down to the arcade of the hotel and from a pay station in a drug store phoned the Fanwick in Sherman and asked for Carl Decker.

"Jervis talking," he said. "Carl, check out, put your luggage on a taxi and drive out to the Mammoth Studios, which I believe are on the other side of Cahuenga Pass."

"Why?" demanded Carlos sharply.

"I'll meet you at the main entrance and tell you. Check out, please, and take all your stuff with you."

"What did you say was the name of this studio?"

"Mammoth."

"With all the pleasure in the world," exclaimed the king.

"Why so much pleasure?"

Carl laughed cheerfully.

"I'll explain to you when I meet you there," he retorted and hung up.

Will scratched his head.

"Now, what in the devil did he mean by that?" he asked himself.

CHAPTER XXIII

THE LEADING WOMAN

THE MAMMOTH FILM CORPORATION occupied a hundred acres of land in the valley beyond the pass, having moved out there from Hollywood when real estate in the film metropolis began to be nearly as expensive as corner lots in Manhattan. The hundred acres was a present to Mammoth, as represented by Mr. Goldsmith, from the Paradise Vale Development Company, which had purchased five thousand acres for a few hundred dollars an acre and proceeded to cut it up into home sites to be sold at ten dollars a front foot.

By no possibility could anything be made to grow upon the soil in Paradise Vale, but the development company laid out streets, installed water mains and other improvements, brought huge rolls of sod from more fertile districts, and constructed lovely green lawns about the decoy houses it proceeded to erect, and for a time did well.

Goldsmith had moved out to the free site, constructed an imposing eight-foot wall of gleaming white around it, which, incidentally, was not as solid as it looked, being built of chicken wire at which workmen had tossed cement. Taking the million which he had received for his tiny studio grounds in Hollywood, he built impressive-looking administration buildings, stages, shops, and such, not much more substantial than the sets which were put up and taken down upon the open lot for temporary use.

Not having wasted money on bricks, steel frames and

masonry, Goldsmith was able to spend a lot for ornamentation. King Carlos was overcome with admiration when he crossed the broad lawns in the center of which fountains were softly plashing and gazed upon the superb white palace in which the executives of Mammoth had their offices. In all Berania there was nothing more beautiful.

Will was already present and met him a few rods from the entrance.

"So this is where they manufacture films!" exclaimed Carlos. "It bears quite a resemblance to the Grand Trianon."

"That's probably from what the artist stole his plan," said Will, smiling. "Carl, you and I are going to live inside these walls for the next three months."

"Eh? Are you mad?"

"Quite sane. We have a large house at our disposal, beautifully furnished, I understand, and the president of the" company is giving us his own cook and valet."

"Kind of him. Why does he do this?"

"In this institution, I think we are reasonably safe from the bullet and the knife. The place is guarded like a prison. Your identity will be scrupulously concealed. It is made to order for our purposes."

"And what are our purposes?" asked the king suspiciously.

"We'll go to our quarters and make ourselves comfortable," proposed Will, "and I'll explain everything. You can rely upon me, can't you?"

Carl clapped him upon the shoulder. "Yes," he said. "I have been relying upon you, more or less, since the day I abdicated."

Jervis beckoned to several young men in lavender uniforms with brass buttons who rushed out to the taxi of the Aronhof, loaded themselves with his suitcases and came toward the pair.

Carl followed his companion across an anteroom, the extreme emptiness of which would have surprised a person accustomed to a crowd waiting to see supervisors, producers, directors or actresses, through a turnstile, down a corridor and into the open air of the lot. Intent upon maintaining secrecy, Goldsmith had given orders that the waiting room be cleared lest there be some one to note the great resemblance of the new actor to King Carlos of Berania.

A guide took them in hand upon the lot and conducted them past a huge warehouse-like, windowless building marked Stage Number Five, through a passage between two similar structures and out upon a smiling expanse of lawn beyond which was a gem-like villa, the garden of which was surrounded with an eight-foot wall.

"Amazing!" exclaimed Carlos.

"Our home," said Will, smiling.

A servant in lavender livery opened the door for them and conducted them into a long vaulted living room furnished with veritable museum pieces.

"I would say that Aladdin had rubbed a ring and his jinni had constructed this," remarked Carlos. "It's beyond words!"

"Do you gentlemen wish to see your chambers?" asked the servant.

"Not now," said Will. "You may go. We wish to be alone."

CARL threw himself upon a divan and Will seated himself in a great throne chair.

"I have made arrangements for you and me to make a motion picture," he said uneasily.

The king sat bolt upright.

"Then you have exhibited unwarranted effrontery," he cried angrily. "I'm damned if I do anything of the kind."

"Why not?" asked Will calmly.

"Why? You forget who I am!"

Jervis had devoted considerable thought to this interview.

"Just who are you?" he asked blandly.

"*Dios!* You should know who I am."

"Recent chauffeur for Mrs. Mason Swasey and this morning released from the city jail. King Carlos of Berania was assassinated in New York yesterday. According to the late afternoon newspapers, the Duke of Burzio has thrown up the sponge and fled to Paris and the royalists have disbanded."

"I thought you were my friend," said the king bitterly.

"Everything has arranged itself nicely for the Torres gang. The oligarchy has been preserved. They can now devote their entire attention to locating you and me and neatly massacring us. Well, they'll have some trouble getting at us here. And, after you have made a few scenes in this picture, Goldsmith will be ready to lay down his life for yours."

"Who is Goldsmith?"

"Well, I am Aladdin. Goldsmith is the jinni I evoked by rubbing my ring. In fact he owns this studio. Quite an interesting person. Originally, I believe, he ran a sewing machine in a cloak and suit factory."

Carl scowled. "Do you expect an Aronhof to turn into an actor?" he demanded sternly.

Will shook his head. "Not a good actor, but adequate. This is the situation. We are going to work in a motion picture. The greatest secrecy will be preserved. It may never be released, but it will be three months in the making and we are reasonably safe from our enemies.

"At the end of three months the situation may be that you might as well be a film actor as anything else. Torres and his crew may be so firmly established that they can dispense with our elimination. Or the better element of Berania may have thrown them out, in which case we shall be able to sleep nights without fear of assassins. Mr. Goldsmith is entitled to some return for his hospitality and they say that making motion pictures is entertaining."

"Bah!" retorted the king. "You have better reasons than that for this absurd arrangement."

Will smiled. "Perhaps. I have a scheme. It's rather nebulous; most likely it will amount to nothing. I have detailed the substantial advantages of being here. But I'm sending a cablegram to-night to a friend of mine in the Paris Legation who will pass it on to the Duke of Burzio."

"If you are still hoping for my recall to Berania, permit me to state that my people would never accept a king who had been a play actor. As I told you this morning, I don't want to go back. By the way, I said I would tell you why I was pleased to visit this studio. Dalma Dawning is working here. I wish to find her now and explain that it was through no fault of mine that I did not keep our engagement last night."

"You can't leave this house, your majesty, except to go guarded to the stage on which we are going to work."

Carl rose resolutely. "I've had enough of this. I am going out now to find Dalma."

"For heaven's sake, be reasonable."

Carl threw back his head and laughed as though he hadn't a care.

"I am," he declared. "I am destroying my last chance of being recalled to Berania by becoming a picture actor. Well, I love a picture actress. I will marry her. Both members of the same cast. What could be more splendid?"

"Frankly, I expect that this film will replace you on your throne. You can't marry her."

"I'll brook no interference in this, Jervis," Carlos said firmly.

"Take it easy," replied Will, laughing. "Sit down. You don't know how powerful we are on this lot. I'll phone Goldsmith and have her sent over for inspection for a rôle in the picture."

"By George!" exclaimed the king. "Can we do that? I consent to be an actor, my friend, if Dalma plays with me."

DALMA DAWNING was sitting on a piano bench in a drawing-room set on stage three in which about forty extra women were being utilized. The star and leading man were in the foreground. Microphone and camera were ready.

"Hit them," somebody shouted, and the scene was immediately flooded with lights. Dalma was not even facing the camera.

She was atmosphere and she was busy with her own thoughts, which were not joyful ones. What had happened to Carl Decker? She didn't have to be told that it was through no fault of his that he had not kept his engagement to see her. Something had happened to him.

At 10 P.M. she had mustered enough courage to phone the Swaseys and ask permission to speak to Mr. Decker.

"He is no longer employed here," the butler had informed her. Her heart gave a leap of satisfaction at that. But if he was not working, what had prevented him from calling on her? It was certain that something must have happened to him. That vile Junior Swasey might have struck at him again, this time successfully. At midnight she had phoned the hospitals.

It was not to be denied that she had fallen madly in love with Carl Decker. Why not? He was handsome, cultured— brave as a menagerie full of lions, as she had ample evidence. And Carl liked her. A girl could tell. Oh, she hoped that nothing had happened to him!

A messenger touched the director on the shoulder and handed him a note. He glanced at it, made a gesture to the radio operator who cut off the "mike" while an assistant director shouted to the light man, "Save 'em," and immediately the great arcs went out.

"Miss Dawning," called the director.

Dalma started violently and looked up in alarm. What could she have done that was wrong?

"Come here, please," commanded the director. "Jones, put another girl on the piano stool."

"Fired," she thought disconsolately. She had expected at least a week's work, and she needed the money.

The director descended from his platform and met her.

"Report at once," he said, "to Mr. Jervis in the Italian villa."

"The villa? Do you know what it is for, Mr. Drake?"

"No," he said shortly. "Important enough to break in on a big scene. Step on it, sister."

With beating heart the little actress made her way across the dusty ground and came in sight of the exquisite residence which was so utterly incongruous upon a motion picture grounds.

She knocked timidly at the door in the wall, and a liveried servant admitted her.

"Mr. Jervis, please," she said.

"Right this way, miss."

SHE FOLLOWED him into the drawing room, hesitated when she saw two men at the far end of the room, and her eyes widened and her cheeks reddened when she recognized Carl Decker, who was coming toward her with outstretched hands.

"Dalma!" he exclaimed. "I'm so glad to see you."

"But, Carl," she said, "how do you happen to be here and what happened to you last night?"

"I was the victim of a plot," he said hurriedly. "Junior Swasey accused me of theft—"

"Oh, the beast!" she exclaimed. "Why didn't you telephone me? I would have told them a few things about Junior Swasey."

Carl shook his head. By this time he had her hands, and she was quite willing to have him hold them.

"I could not have had you mixed up in it, my dear," he said. "I spent the night in jail, but my friend, Mr. Jervis, secured my release this morning. This is Mr. Jervis, Miss Dawning."

Dalma turned to Will with a grateful smile.

"It is a pleasure to meet any friend of Carl's," she said. "Do you know, Carl, I was afraid he might frame you in some way. I—I phoned, late last night, to Swasey's and was told that you were no longer employed there."

Will's sharp eyes were scrutinizing the girl as she spoke, and what he saw pleased him. The lovely little creature was no movie milkmaid. She had patrician features, her speech was free of vulgarities, her tone was sweet and clear. If he had not heard her express herself in the American vernacular without a trace of accent, he would have assumed her a North European.

That she was in love with Carl Decker was as evident from the look in her eyes as it was obvious that he was mad about her. It was a pity, Will thought. This little girl had depth and infinite capacity for suffering, and there could be no happy ending to the love affair.

She gave him her hand, and, as he took it, he noticed that she wore a heavy gold ring with a curiously carved stone of blue flecked with gold. His eyes gleamed with interest. It was a man's ring, of no great value, for the stone was Russian lapis lazuli.

"I am very glad to meet you," he said gravely. "By the way, are you aware that that's an unusual ring you have there?"

"It's old," she replied, "but not worth much. It belonged to my father."

"I wonder if you would let me look at it."

She slipped it from her finger and handed it to him indifferently as she turned back to Carl.

"Anyway," she said, "you are not a chauffeur any longer."

Will walked to a window, drew from his pocket a small magnifying glass, and studied the setting of the ring. The stone had been carved to serve as a seal and the seal was the head of a bear.

He sucked in his breath sharply, pocketed his magnifying glass and rejoined the others.

"A very interesting ring," he said. "Do you know how old it is?"

"I know it is very old. I was told to report to you, Mr. Jervis. Are you a supervisor?"

"No," he said, smiling. "I suppose I am an author. I'm writing a motion picture in which Mr. Decker is to play an important rôle."

"Really?" she exclaimed. "Carl, you know I told you that you should go in for pictures."

"It appears that you were right," Carl said solemnly. "I'm going to play a king, it appears."

She clapped her hands. "Oh, you'll be marvelous."

"Mr. Jervis has persuaded me," he informed her.

"It's like this, Miss Dawning," said Will. "A big film dealing very largely with the recent events in Berania is to be made by this company. Confidentially, Mr. Goldsmith had engaged the ex-King Carlos to play the rôle, but he was assassinated, as you know. The company is obliged to make the picture notwithstanding, and I happened to know that Mr. Decker looks very much like the ex-King of Berania. I have persuaded him on condition that you will play the leading feminine rôle."

DALMA grew white and for a second it looked as though she would faint.

"But—but—I've never played a big part," she protested.

"Yet you could if you had the opportunity."

"Ye-es. I think so."

"Tell me something about yourself."

"There is nothing to tell."

"Where do your parents live?"

"My father is dead. My mother remarried. I do not like my stepfather. That's why I came out here to go into pictures."

"How long ago did your father die?"

"About ten years ago."

"Please give me your mother's address. You may have to take chances in this picture. I wish it as a precaution."

"I don't mind taking chances. My mother is Mrs. Ralph P. Grady, and her address is 1919 Greening Street, Chicago."

"Thank you. Now, you will please not mention having met Mr. Decker here to-day. You will tell nobody that he is making this picture. He and I will live in this house and not leave the studio until the film is finished. It will be made under unusually secretive conditions. Mr. Decker will appear personally only in certain close-ups and intimate scenes, and another actor will double for him in long shots and in the big spectacular scenes. You are the only person who knows that he is in the studio and you'll have to be most discreet."

"I shall. Oh, I shall."

"I'll arrange with Mr. Goldsmith for a contract for you at a good salary, and you can consider the matter settled."

"But you'll have to make tests of me."

"You have been appearing in pictures. You have been tested, haven't you?"

"Yes, but not for a leading rôle."

"We'll take a chance on you," he said, smiling. "I'm going to leave you children alone for a few minutes. I am delighted to have met you."

"What a wonderful person!" exclaimed Dalma when she was alone with Carl. "It seems to me that I have heard his name and seen his picture somewhere. Is he a very great author?"

"I guess so," said Carl. "Let's talk about us. Dalma, I'm going to ask you a question. If this thing works out so that it is possible, will you marry me?"

She blushed. "You put it so strangely. Why should it be impossible?"

"I can't explain, dear. I just want you to know that I love you, whatever happens. I'm mixed up in curious circumstances, dear."

"I don't care what the circumstances are," she said bravely. "I know that you are incapable of wrongdoing; that there is nothing shameful. Carl—you are not married?"

"I certainly am not."

"That's all that matters. Carl!"

When Will returned they were in each other's arms and they faced him openly.

"So that's the way it is," he commented good naturedly.

"This is the way it is," said Carl firmly. "I have proposed to Dalma and she has accepted me."

"When are you going to be married?" Jervis asked blandly.

"As soon as possible."

"Which will not be until this job is done, Miss Dawning," said Will sternly.

CHAPTER XXIV

CONSPIRATORS

MLLE. LEFEVRE, OR Reine de la Reine as she was registered at the Ambassador, was seated at the window of her sitting room reading an English novel when her telephone rang.

"Torres," said a male voice laconically.

"*Bien.* Come up," she replied in a suddenly agitated tone.

The first of her visitors Jervis would have recognized as the handsome blond man he had seen in the company of the late Alfonso Gomez in the theater loge upon the night when Will was visited by Count Grandez and his assassins. The other was smaller, with beady black eyes and an olive skin.

Each kissed the small white hand of the young woman and accepted the chairs to which she motioned them.

"*Mademoiselle,* you are more beautiful than ever," said the blond man. "Did I not tell you, Señor Flores, that you would meet the most beautiful Beranian woman living?"

The dark man bowed gallantly.

"You need not have qualified your description by nationality," he said. "*Mademoiselle,* I am at your feet."

"Thank you, gentlemen. You have given me the password. I have been expecting Señor Galbo. It is a pleasure to meet Señor Flores. And now to business."

"Your mission has been successful?" asked Galbo.

The young woman rose, unlocked a small bag and from it produced the decoration of the Order of the Lion of Berania.

Galbo accepted it reverently and said:

"Carlos committed a crime in bestowing it upon Jervis after he was dethroned."

"For no other reason would I have undertaken the mission," said the young woman. "But, since making the acquaintance of Mr. Jervis, I feel sure that such measures were unnecessary. He is a gentleman. He would have returned the decoration if requested by the government of Berania."

"Jervis," declared Galbo, "is the mortal enemy of Berania. Permit me, *mademoiselle*."

He drew five one-thousand-dollar bank notes from a wallet and presented them to Mlle. LeFevre. She accepted them with obvious reluctance.

"**I HAVE** bitterly regretted having undertaken this mission," Mlle. LeFevre declared. "Only my great need persuaded me to descend to what is hardly less than burglary."

"You have performed a wonderful service for your country, *mademoiselle*," declared Galbo, who rose and saluted her as he spoke. Flores did likewise.

"I wonder," she said with a sigh. "Berania seems even less happy under the republic."

"Because we came into power and found the treasury looted, the crown jewels purloined and our hands tied for lack of money due to the criminal whose name is Aronhof."

"Let us not speak ill of the dead," said the girl with spirit. "As kings go, Carlos did not seem to be a bad example."

The two men exchanged glances and Galbo nodded.

"You are right," he declared.

"You will cable immediately to release Mme. Reine de la Reine?" she asked earnestly.

"She is very comfortable," he replied. "She is in the Convent of Saint Theresa and the abbess has special instructions that she will lack for nothing. We shall have to detain her for a few weeks longer, for you can still be useful to us, *mademoiselle*."

"In what manner?"

"You are friendly with this Jervis. He does not suspect you?"

Her color rose. "I think not," she said in a low tone.

"It is very important for us to locate him. We find that he arrived at this hotel several hours before you did, but he checked out the same day and left no address."

"Why do you wish to find him? Why should Berania be interested in him further?"

"It is not necessary for you to know our reasons," said Galbo stiffly.

The girl's tiny foot began to tap the carpet.

"You can trust me. I am a patriotic Beranian," she declared.

"If you were not, the government would not have made use of you," he replied coldly. "We had need of a beautiful woman agent in America. Fortune favored us by the acceptance of a motion picture contract by Reine de la Reine. With her credentials we brought you to this country, supplied you amply with money, have liberally rewarded you for the successful accomplishment of your first mission and we have a right to expect further assistance from you. I may add that you will be well paid for further services also."

"I like Mr. Jervis," she said. "I feel degraded at having robbed him even of a trinket to which he has no right and which can be of no use to him. You must convince me that you have no evil intentions toward him."

FLORES smiled significantly at his colleague.

"How like a woman," he declared. "This man is dangerous. We must keep him under observation."

"In what way is he dangerous? He was the friend of King Carlos, but Carlos is dead. How can he harm us?"

"He might produce a false Carlos," said Galbo smoothly. "Remember that the world knows that he was intimate with the late king. These Yankees will do anything for gain."

"Nonsense," she said scornfully. "Mr. Jervis is a gentleman. I am certain that he will have no further interest in the government of Berania since Carlos has perished."

"Our orders are to keep him under surveillance. You are beautiful. You can gain his confidence. You can do this work better than we."

"I am a gentlewoman," she replied. "I refuse to do anything underhanded."

Galbo bowed. "Very well, but tell us where he can be found."

She shrugged. "Oh, for that matter, he is on the Mammoth lot."

"The film company? What is he doing there?"

"I believe he is acting in an advisory capacity in connection with a picture they are making, based upon the life story of King Carlos."

"But that picture has been abandoned. Carlos was to play himself and he is dead."

"They are very secretive at Mammoth," she replied, "but rumors get around. I've heard that the picture will be made and they have found an actor who will play the king. Mr. Goldsmith was on the train with both Jervis and myself and he urged him to play in the film the rôle he played in the escape of Carlos. At the time Jervis refused, but he must have reconsidered, for I saw him from my window at the studio yesterday walking across the lot... What's the matter?"

She had become aware that they were listening in menacing silence.

"You must find a way to talk with him and discover exactly what he is doing," commanded Galbo. "This is a matter of life and death. We must not fail in it." Galbo and Flores were staring at each other with tense, strained faces.

CHAPTER XXV

A SPY TURNS HER COAT

"WHAT ON EARTH does it matter to Berania?" Mlle. LeFevre demanded.

"The *señorita* is as good a patriot as we are," Flores told Galbo hastily. "She has the entrée to this studio. We must take her into our confidence."

"You are heart and soul for the republic?" Galbo questioned her.

"But of course."

"Very well. There is grave danger of a huge royalist uprising. One rumor, one whisper that Carlos is alive, and the country will blaze, *señorita*."

"Well?"

"Who is this actor who is to play with Jervis in this film?"

"It is kept a secret. It is very curious. They say he is living in a cottage on the studio grounds and nobody but Mr. Goldsmith is permitted to see him."

"You will take us with you into the studio and we shall see him," said Galbo excitedly.

"Impossible. No one can enter without a special pass. I cannot bring in people. I cannot visit any part of the grounds except where my own building is located. There is the greatest mystery surrounding the work which is being done there."

"Is the place guarded?"

She nodded. "There are scores of watchmen, some of them armed."

"All on account of this cursed film?"

"No. They guard all their pictures in this manner. They are terrified of spies from other studios."

"Well," said Flores, "you must steal us a copy of the scenario of this film which deals with King Carlos."

She laughed. "Still more impossible. Stories are their gold. There is no possibility that I could read any story except that upon which I am working. And even there I do not expect to be able to deceive them very long. I am not a writer of fiction. In a week or two weeks at the most they will dispense with my services."

"Then you must learn what we wish to know from Jervis."

"I hate myself for ever consenting to be the tool of unscrupulous men," she cried passionately. "I worked earnestly for the republic and what do I find when the king has been dethroned? A military dictatorship! Do you suppose a real republic would pursue an innocent alien into the heart of his own country? I believe, oh, now I am certain that this alleged republic murdered King Carlos in New York."

"You are so greatly mistaken, *señorita,*" replied Galbo gravely, "that you will be amazed when I tell you the truth. So far from the facts is your surmise that I will confide to you that royalists killed the man in New York because they knew he was not King Carlos. Carlos is not dead."

THE GIRL turned very pale and her great eyes seemed to grow even larger.

"Not dead?" she gasped.

"Not dead. While he lives, he is a menace to Berania. He is biding his time. He hides and Jervis knows where he is. That is why we are interested in Jervis."

"There is no doubt in my mind," added Flores, "that the man who lives in a cottage in the grounds of your picture company is Carlos Aronhof. He and Jervis plot mischief together. We are patriots, *señorita.* No republic can function while Carlos is alive. The military dictatorship is forced upon our people."

The armed mob surged forward.

"We have absolute information that Carlos is in Los Angeles and that Jervis came out here to join him," said Galbo. "Will you let your sympathy for this American betray your country?"

"No," said the girl. "No. Certainly not. But you are not going to kill the king?"

"We are not murderers. We wish to capture him and keep him confined so that he can do no mischief."

She sighed. "Very well. I shall do what I can."

"This film company is located in a lonely spot in the valley beyond the Cahuenga Pass, I believe." said Galbo.

She nodded.

"And a few hours in an automobile and one is across the border into Mexico. Very good. Your immediate duty is to gain the confidence of this man. Jervis. The watchword is still Torres. We bid you *au revoir, señorita.*"

"Au revoir," she said in a low tone.

When she found herself alone, the lovely young political

agent went into her bedroom and threw herself upon the bed. She lay upon her back with her hands pressed hard against her eyes and for a long time she was motionless while her mind was busy with that part of her life which was responsible for the situation in which she found herself.

Aimee LeFevre was the daughter of a French father and Beranian mother. She was born in Madrova and attended a convent there until her eighteenth year when her mother died and her father moved to Paris and took her with him. She was an unusually intelligent girl and her father indulged her. He permitted her to become a student at the Sorbonne where she associated with liberals from every nation and became fired with the idea of republicanizing Berania, which she considered her native land. When she was twenty-two her father died, leaving her a small income, and she returned to Madrova where she soon became the moving spirit in a woman's republican club.

Although Berania was almost an absolute monarchy, King Carlos himself was a liberal and made little effort to throttle free speech. For a couple of years Aimee LeFevre worked feverishly for the republic and overnight it was born.

It did not take the clever girl long to appreciate, however, that the new government was republican only in name. The group of unprincipled men who grasped power had no intention of risking defeat in a general election. A secret police was established and those who talked loudest for freedom began to disappear from public view.

AIMEE had given a lecture on true representative government upon a certain evening and had worked her audience into a frenzy of excitement. As she was leaving the hall she was accosted by two army officers who informed her that General Torres wished to see her immediately and placed her in an automobile which conducted her to the palace.

It was evident to her that she was headed for prison like

other ardent and indiscreet republicans, but, to her surprise, the provisional president treated her with great consideration.

He explained to her most courteously that the bulk of the nation was royalist at heart and that the suddenness of the revolt had taken the peasantry by surprise or it would have failed.

"Had King Carlos made a fight of it," he said, "the country folks would have flocked to his standard. Half the army was loyal. It was likely that his majesty would have triumphed. The provisional government is forced to be dictatorial. A true republic is impossible while there is a possibility of Carlos returning. He is supposed to be in the United States, but his whereabouts are unknown. A watch must be kept upon him so that any overt move might be foreseen and guarded against."

Already a number of loyal and able Beranians had filtered into the United States to work in the interest of the republic, he said, but a woman agent of her ability was greatly needed. Carlos must be kept in America for at least a year. By that time republican principles would have made sufficient headway and he would no longer be a danger. Was she willing to support her words with action? Would she go to America?

Knowing that a refusal would mean her probable incarceration, she consented to go.

Torres explained that the Beranian quota for admission to America was full, but arrangements would be made for her admission. Reine de la Reine, the famous French novelist who lived in Madrova, had been offered a contract by a motion picture company in Los Angeles. Aimee would go in her stead. When she arrived in New York she would be given specific instructions. The password was Torres.

Aimee had enjoyed the voyage thoroughly and was thrilled by the adventure of New York. She carried off the interview with the New York representatives of Mammoth Films very successfully. They had not the slightest suspicion that she was not what she pretended and they were delighted that she was younger and more beautiful than they dared to hope.

Goldsmith, president of the company, happened to be in New York, met her, and was smitten with her. He was leaving for Hollywood in a few days, and impudently suggested that she make the trip West with him, a suggestion which she knew how to turn down without offending him.

What was her astonishment and dismay when she received her first assignment! Galbo called upon her, gave the password, presented her with reservations for Los Angeles upon a certain train, and instructed her to make the acquaintance of the American, William Jervis, and, in whatever manner seemed best to her, to get the decoration of the Lion of Berania.

Her protests were unavailing. She boarded the train. Upon the first morning chance introduced her to Jervis, whom she liked better than any other man she had ever met—before he told her his name.

To complicate matters, she found herself upon the train which Goldsmith had urged her to take, and he jumped at the conclusion that she was aboard to be complaisant.

She had seized her opportunity to enter Jervis's drawing room and recover the Lion of Berania, and, according to instructions, she had left the train at the next stop. She was utterly miserable. While she was a patriot, she was not a thief.

It was not until she encountered Will at the Ambassador Hotel that she learned from his lips that he was the target of the marksmen upon the station platform, and she shrewdly put two and two together. The assassination of the man in New York whom she assumed to be King Carlos and the attempt upon the life of bis American friend came too close together not to be part of the same plot, and the plotters were the people with whom she was allied.

SHE HAD committed only one crime in her life; the purloining of the golden lion from the luggage of Will Jervis. She considered political assassination as horrible as any other kind of murder. While the welfare of the Beranian republic might be construed by fanatics to require the elimination of Carlos, there was no reason in the world why a splendid young American like Jervis should be killed, and she thanked God on her knees for sparing his life.

She was in a very serious predicament, however. She was an impostor who would be ejected from the film studio and perhaps jailed if her masquerade were discovered, and she was dependent upon the Beranian conspirators. If she turned on them, it was not likely that her life would be safe. She determined, however, to accept no more disreputable commissions, and, if the opportunity came to her, she would confess to Jervis her crime against him and try to make him understand her predicament.

It was that day that Jervis moved into the cottage on the Mammoth lot. Aimee reported at the studio, and Goldsmith, enamored as ever, broke his word to Jervis regarding keeping her off the lot and gave her a tiny office in the administration building upon the same corridor as his own.

Several days passed, and then came the visit from the Beranian conspirators. Her attitude had forced them to take her to a certain extent into their confidence, but the effect of their revelations upon her was quite different from what they had anticipated.

Aimee had closely followed the situation in Berania and knew the seriousness of the royalist revolt. If the man in New York was not the king, he must be an agent of the Torres government like herself. He had been assassinated immediately after the royalists had won a big battle, and the receipt of the news in Berania had caused the revolt to collapse.

This meant to Aimee that Torres, finding himself in a fight place, had ordered the murder of his own agent. She grew sick thinking about it.

And to continue to sustain himself in power he would have to hunt down the real Aronhof and kill him, and with him Carlos's friend, Jervis, the American.

Both Carlos and Jervis were living secretly in the cottage at

Mammoth and were making a motion picture. What purpose such a picture might serve them was beyond the comprehension of Aimee LeFevre.

When a woman's emotions are engaged she reasons with her heart. It became immediately plain to Aimee that the oligarchy which ruled Berania was much more to be hated than the kindly young monarch who had been dethroned. And the establishment of a real republic in her country had been retarded instead of accomplished by the uprising which had planted Torres and his crew in the royal palace.

Carlos had been a good king according to his lights. If he were restored to the throne, he would probably agree to make the Chamber of Representatives really representative. A good constitutional monarchy was better than a bad republic.

Then and there Aimee LeFevre turned her coat and did not even admit to herself that her fundamental reason was personified by the brave and agreeable young American, Will Jervis.

CHAPTER XXVI

JERVIS HEARS A CONFESSION

ISIDORE GOLDSMITH SAT in his gold and white office at a veritable Louis XIV desk and wagged his head dolefully over a manuscript.

"I ought to have known better," he declared. "I never done no business with amateurs before, and I had no business starting."

"What's the matter?" asked Will Jervis, smiling.

"It's the rottenest story that I ever read in my life," declared the magnate. "I'll have to call in a few good authors and see what we can do about it."

"I will confer with your director regarding best methods of shooting it," replied Will, "but this is the story we are going to make, if we make any."

"You got this king quitting right in the first scene," protested Goldsmith. "There won't be any sympathy for him. He's got to go out and get licked in a big battle."

"Wrong. The whole world will sympathize with a king who gives up his throne to save his country from civil war."

"Well, this business about his being a chauffeur. That's out. It ain't reasonable."

"It is very important. That is how he meets the girl. She recognized the prince beneath the livery of the chauffeur."

"Like heck she would. Anyway, it's almost all in America. I want a lot of foreign color."

"You can get all you want in the first and last reels."

"But this double business. Nobody believes in doubles any more. And you got the government of this country killing its own man. That ain't logical."

"Very well," said Will rising. "This may be a bad picture. I doubt if it will be the first bad picture you have made."

"Oh, as for that, lots of 'em are duds."

"And you must remember that, in this, you have a crowned king as leading man. Even if it is a terrible story, the chance to see King Carlos in a picture will pack your theaters, won't it?"

"But I'd rather have a good story."

Will laughed. "This is all you're going to get."

Goldsmith scowled, tapped nervously upon his desk, and finally pressed a button.

"All right," he said. "We'll shoot the damn thing as is. After all, we don't have to put this here king out in a follow-up film."

FROM the standpoint of secrecy, the method of making talking pictures is very nearly ideal. Scenes are rarely shot in sequence. Most of the scenes which unfold the plot are played by a few principals with only cameramen and sound operators for audience.

The director found Will Jervis his greatest bane, for Jervis was a bad actor and had tremendous difficulty with his lines though he had written them himself. King Carlos was a born actor; to be a king one must be a natural Thespian, and he played his rôle almost as skillfully as the most experienced male star in Hollywood. As for Dalma Dawning, she was a "natural" in the opinion of the director. Carlos might be a one-picture star but this film would make the leading woman.

As the big sets had been constructed and were waiting to be used, the picture moved with unusual rapidity. At the end of two weeks it was two-thirds done, and Goldsmith, looking at the rushes nightly in the living room of the Italian villa in the company of Jervis and Carlos, began to be enthusiastic. He was getting considerable kick out of being chummy with a king, and was in a state of mind where a much worse picture than that which was in the making would have appeared good to him.

Carl privately bemoaned his situation and protested earnestly to his friend against this indecent exposure of his private life.

"We have the veto power," Will assured him often. "If, when it is finished, we decide that we do not want it to go out, we can prevent them from showing it. In the meantime, we are in sanctuary. It's three weeks since anybody has fired a shot at me."

Carlos smiled. "That is so," he admitted. "It is temporary safety, but the time will come when we shall have to leave this fantastic institution. The chief objection I have is playing the rôle of the scoundrel Gomez, as well as my own. Can't we cut that part of it out?"

"Wait until the whole picture is finished," pleaded Will. "We can cut out anything we like."

Carl laughed. "That rogue who is playing General Torres is marvelous. I feel an almost irresistible impulse to shoot him whenever I see him. Lucky I have no bullets in my revolver."

"He is the best heavy in motion pictures. It would be a pity to kill him," said Will, smiling. "By the way, the Duke of Burzio is again in Sepoia."

"Nothing in the world would induce me to go back to Berania," declared Carlos. "You know why. I have written to Burzio in care of your friend in the embassy in Paris telling him that he must not lift my standard again."

"It's a crime to leave Torres to misgovern your country."

"My country preferred him to me," said Carl stiffly. "Let us not speak of this again."

Will thoughtfully tapped a letter in his pocket. It was addressed to the Duke of Burzio in Carl's handwriting and had not gone into the mails.

The final scene in the film was a great spectacle which depicted the return in triumph of the exile to his throne in response to a spontaneous demand of his people. One thousand extras were to be used and the public square in front of the royal palace was the set. As there was no longer need for secrecy, King Carlos, in person, would appear in the scene and the entire resources of the studio were to be used.

To the delight of Goldsmith, whose contracts permitted him three months in which to produce the picture, the director was ready to shoot this scene upon the twenty-first day.

Jervis, who had forced the story upon him and stuck to his guns from the beginning to the end, had frequent conferences with the producer as the finish drew near, and spent more and more time in the administration building. Upon the afternoon before the great spectacle was scheduled, he left Goldsmith's office and was petrified to find himself confronted, in the corridor, by Mademoiselle LeFevre.

Hard work had not put the girl entirely out of his mind, but he had come most reluctantly to the conclusion that she was a Beranian spy and his enemy. Therefore the radiant, colorful beauty of her dazzled him, when encountered unexpectedly, even more forcibly than it had when he first saw her on the observation platform of the train.

"MADEMOISELLE—" he stammered.

"M. Jervis, I must speak to you," she said eagerly. "Please, just step into this room.

"In the first place," she said, coloring furiously, "I must confess to you that—that—"

"That you looted my luggage on the train," he said grimly.

"How did you know?" she faltered.

"Your perfume. 'Cœur d'Eros.'"

She gasped. "You—you are clever," she murmured.

"I don't care anything about the decoration," he said, "but it hurt me to think that you, whom I admired so much—"

She clasped her hands together nervously. "Please. I am in the depths of humiliation. I assure you that I acted—"

"You, of course, are a Beranian agent," he said. "I suspected it from the first."

"I am. I was. I am a patriot, M. Jervis. I love my country."

"I understand. You have a government of murderers, *mademoiselle*."

"I swear I didn't know until a few days ago how fiendishly unscrupulous they were. I am on your side, now, M. Jervis."

"I am pleased to hear it," he said guardedly.

"Oh, I shall convince you," she said eagerly. "I know, for example, that King Carlos is alive and is here on this lot with you."

"You are in error," he replied much perturbed.

"Some day, perhaps, I shall tell you my history and you, I hope, will forgive me for what I have done. I assure you I did not realize the kind of people with whom I was associated. That they should have tried to kill you! I was filled with horror when I learned that." Her earnestness was making an impression upon a man who yearned to be convinced of her honesty.

"Since I have learned that his majesty is not dead, I have become a royalist," she declared. "I wish to serve him."

"Indeed."

She smiled pathetically. "You do not trust me. Yet I shall probably lose my life because of what I am going to reveal to you."

"By God, they won't harm you," he exclaimed. *"Mademoiselle,* I want to believe you. I never met a girl before whom I wished so much to trust."

"I shall persuade you," she said, smiling. "Now, *monsieur,* listen while I betray my former associates."

She lowered her voice and spoke rapidly for several minutes. Will listened in growing astonishment.

"Now, what can you do?" she asked anxiously.

"Thanks to you, I think we can do quite a little. I'm worried about you, though. How do you happen to be in the studio? Goldsmith promised me not to admit you until our work was over."

"I have been here every day," she replied. "M. Goldsmith is rather charmed by me, I think."

"You will be here to-morrow, then?"

"Yes, as usual."

"I'll ask Goldsmith to have you conducted immediately to the cottage. I don't know how to repay you."

She smiled wistfully. "Perhaps, in time, you will find a way, *monsieur.*"

He offered her his hand. She hesitated, then laid her little hand in his.

"No longer enemies," he said, smiling.

"Allies," she declared. "Tell me, *monsieur,* was I so transparent that you suspected me from the first?"

"It happens that I know Reine de la Reine, who is old enough to be your mother. How did she enter into this conspiracy?"

"Poor woman! They placed her in a convent and are keeping her there until they consider that my usefulness to them and the republic is over. *Au revoir,* M. Jervis."

"Until to-morrow morning."

CHAPTER XXVII

THE BATTLE FOR THE VILLA

THE NEXT DAY dawned bright and fair, as is customary in California, and at a quarter before eight a multitude, in every sort of moving contraption from busses to bicycles, came over the pass from Hollywood and invaded the sequestered valley occupied only by the studio and the very few houses of the defunct development company.

From the central casting office came four or five hundred extra men and women who furnished their own transportation. In trucks provided by the studio arrived swarms of Mexican laborers collected by the Mammoth casting office at three dollars a day and delighted, for a brief period, to wear a bright uniform and to perform before the camera.

Upon the back lot, a faithful representation of the Royal Square in Madrova had been standing for weeks. It had already been used for the revolution scene and plot incidents enacted upon it had been cleverly inserted in the news reel pictures of the actual revolt in Berania. Now it was to figure in a scene which had not yet occurred in Madrova: the return of the exiled ruler.

An army of electricians, property men, carpenters, sound men and light and camera men were working there under the eyes of half a dozen assistant directors.

Long lines of people standing before the various windows of the wardrobe department passed in to the attendants the slips supplied them upon their passage through the studio gates and received in exchange the required costumes.

Much experience has trained the studio people to handle mobs expeditiously and expertly. Despite the multitude of one-day actors, there was no confusion. From the wardrobe department, arms filled with bundles, the extras moved steadily toward the long low building equipped as dressing quarters for extra people.

There is caste even among extras and the unsavory looking mob of Mexicans and half-breeds were held in a roped-off area until the others had been served. One of the roughly dressed laborers drew from his pocket a gold watch and surreptitiously consulted it The hour was eight fifteen. He produced a police whistle and blew a lusty blast.

There was a sudden surging of the mob. Men were leaping over the ropes.

"Hey, you Mexes, get back there," shouted a uniformed attendant.

A revolver shot rang out and the unfortunate official fell to the ground.

Over the ropes piled twenty men, fifty, a hundred, and each man had a revolver in his hand.

"This way," shouted the fellow who had blown the whistle and whom Aimee would have recognized as the gallant Señor Flores.

Followed by his mob, he rushed down a narrow lane between two long windowless stage buildings. Behind him he left panic. The bulk of the Mexican laborers were bellowing with excitement and alarm. The shot had caused studio attachés to come running from every direction. Windows went up in the administration building, and a head appeared at every window.

Women began to scream without being aware of why they were screaming, but in a couple of minutes a tremendous burst of firing justified their terror.

The swarm of armed men had debouched from the narrow

lane and were charging across the grass plot in front of the Italian villa. Four of the Mexicans were carrying a piece of heavy timber they had been directed by Flores to pick up en route, and immediately headed for the door in the wall surrounding the house while the others opened up and spread like a fan to cover the men with the battering ram. The villa lay tranquil. The coup could not fail.

AND THE BERANIAN agents had planned shrewdly. Unable to penetrate the studio under ordinary conditions, the necessity of a huge mob of Mexicans for the big spectacle had given them their opportunity. As Yates had warned Jervis weeks before, the proximity of Mexico to Los Angeles permitted the importation of desperate men, and Galbo and Flores were fully aware of that.

The call for the mob had been sent out four days ahead, which gave them time to bring up a score of ex-bandits and discharged Mexican soldiers, while they had drawn from the Mexican quarter of Los Angeles other scores of criminals and cutthroats. These offered their services to the studio casting officials, and Flores arranged, in case any of his followers were rejected, to buy off innocent laborers who were chosen and to substitute his own rascals.

Aware that King Carlos and Will Jervis were living in the villa upon the studio grounds, the plan was to rush the building, slay the pair whose existence was always a menace to General Torres, and be off and away before the Los Angeles police could possibly reach the remote studio.

Although the Beranian hirelings were outnumbered twenty to one by the studio people, Galbo was certain that very few of the latter were armed, and he anticipated no trouble from them. Five minutes in a speeding motor car would bring himself and Flores to an airplane which would land them in Mexico in two hours, while their followers would scatter, relying upon the fact that, unless a Mexican laborer is caught in the act of committing a crime, it was almost impossible to identify him from his fellows.

A uniformed policeman appeared on the wall.

"Drop that timber," he shouted. "What do you men want?"

His answer came in the form of a dozen revolver shots, and with howls and bellows the mob dashed forward, firing wildly and determined to take the place in a single rush.

At that moment there appeared upon the roof of the nearest stage building two men with motion picture cameras, while at an upper window of the villa a third camera suddenly appeared.

When the bearers of the battering ram were within a dozen paces of the door in the wall, it flew open and revealed the muzzle of a machine gun with an armored shield behind which crouched two police operators.

"Disperse, rioters," shouted an unseen voice through an amplifier. The answer was a burst of firing, but the men with the battering ram dropped it and dived out of range of the machine gun.

"Over the wall," shouted Flores in Spanish.

As the wall was only eight feet high, it was easy to scale, but before a single man was over, the big door of the stage building behind them, and two hundred feet distant, slid aside and a machine gun opened with its sinister rattle upon the backs of the mob. And the gun in the villa doorway snarled viciously and spat fire.

The battle was over then and there. The shock troops turned tail and rushed for the passageway between the stage buildings through which they had advanced, but recoiled when they discovered it was occupied by a platoon of police.

"Throw down your arms," came through the amplifier at the villa. "Surrender or we'll kill you to the last man."

Half a dozen revolver shots replied and the police opened fire from the passageway.

Already most of the Mexicans held their arms above their heads. Dozens of them threw themselves flat on the ground to avoid the cross fire, and a few had fallen with bullets in their bodies.

"Form in line," commanded the mysterious voice. "Throw down your weapons."

There was instant obedience. Even Flores did not hesitate, counting upon his own dark skin and black eyes to enable him to pass for a Mexican. It was obvious to him that he had been betrayed. The plan was perfect, but Carlos and Jervis had been fully informed of it and permitted him to lead his little army into a magnificent ambush.

FROM the villa there filed out a long line of uniformed policemen. From the passageway came half a hundred, and from the big door of the stage building filed another score of Los Angeles's finest.

Had they chosen to do so, they could have mowed down the entire storming party, but, counting upon the success of their arrangements, they killed and wounded only a dozen. The fire of both machine guns had been carefully misdirected and a horrible massacre avoided.

In five minutes the Mexicans stood in a long, melancholy line, every man wearing a pair of handcuffs.

"There is a man named Leon Flores among you," said the amplifier. "Let him step forward."

Flores looked startled, but was careful not to move out of the line.

"Have these men identify their leader," commanded the mysterious voice.

With alacrity a score of manacled hands lifted and pointed at the Beranian, who was hustled across the lawn and pushed through the villa entrance.

"You may take the rest of them away," instructed the amplifier.

In the living room of the villa, Isidore Goldsmith rubbed his hands.

"We ain't lost much time," he declared. "It's only eight forty-five. We can go right along with the big scene."

"I think we can fit this battle scene into the film very nicely," said Will Jervis.

"A real live battle with machine guns and everything right in my own studio!" exclaimed the producer. "And people killed, too. Nobody ever got anything like this before."

"It's a pity that we had to shoot any of the poor devils," said Will. "I hoped the machine guns would cause them to throw down their arms."

Goldsmith shrugged his shoulders. "It ain't our fault, and it makes a better shot," he declared. "Oi, what would have happened here if we had not been tipped off? Where's his majesty?"

"Where he usually is, with Dalma Dawning."

"Zowie! What an ad for the film," declared Goldsmith, who could only see the bright side of the unfortunate occurrence. "We get on the front page of every newspaper in the country, Jervis. For a million I couldn't buy the advertising we're going to get."

"Can't we call off the final scene until to-morrow?" asked Will. "Men have been killed out there, Goldsmith."

"Say, it would cost us fifteen thousand dollars to delay a day with everybody on the scene."

"But you've just made a million in advertising," Will reminded him.

"Ye-es, but how do we know what else these murderers have up their sleeve? Get the whole picture in the box and lose no time."

"You're right, at that," admitted Jervis.

A policeman entered.

"We have the leader of this mob outside," he said.

"Wait until I notify *mademoiselle*," said Will to Goldsmith. "You have him brought in and ask him any sort of questions. I'll have her identify him unseen by him."

Flores, soldierly and defiant in his ill-fitting clothes, was pushed into the room, while Will and Aimee peered at him from behind portières which concealed the adjoining room.

"It is Flores," she said. "Galbo is a big blond man. I doubt if he could have passed as a Mexican."

"Flores will do for our purposes," said Will grimly. "He is responsible for the killings here, and we'll squeeze enough facts out of him to round up all the Beranian assassins in the United States. Perhaps we can pin these outrages directly upon Torres by his confession."

"Do you believe now that I am on your side?" asked Aimee wistfully. "Do you forgive me?"

"And how!" cried Will enthusiastically.

CHAPTER XXVIII

A ROYALIST COUP

UPON A CERTAIN night in Madrova, three weeks after the affair at the Mammoth studios in Los Angeles, the usual capacity audience was assembled in the Theatro Libro, formerly the Royal Theater, a great structure which accommodated three thousand spectators. They had assembled to see a famous American woman star in her latest photoplay.

The overture had been played, one or two short subjects had been shown, and at that moment a band of armed men entered the lobby of the theater and quietly took possession of it. There was no disturbance, and the film operators in the booth at the back of the balcony became aware that all was not as usual only when two masked men entered with revolvers and carrying a tin box.

"You will show this as an extra added attraction," said one of these intruders who displayed his weapon significantly. "Where is your announcement amplifier?"

The frightened operator mutely pointed to the instrument, and the stranger took his place before it while his colleague aided the operators to remove the contents of the can.

"Ladies and gentlemen," said the amplifier, "the management has arranged to show you, without extra charge, a remarkable film just arrived from America which will not only entertain but enlighten and astonish you."

Immediately there flashed upon the screen a title: "A King Who Loved His People."

The dumfounded audience looked immediately into the council chamber of King Carlos of Berania. They heard the discussion of the republican rising and they saw their king, in person, and heard him say that he preferred to lose his throne rather than cause the slaughter of his subjects in a civil war.

They saw him write his abdication. They saw him leave the palace and go to the landing field where he met Jervis, the American. And they followed the airplane which bore him to Paris.

Then General Torres came into the picture. While Torres was a scoundrel, the man himself was a polished rogue and he did not exude the villainy which was revealed to them by the sterling heavy who played that rôle.

They listened entranced, if frightened, to the plot to charge King Carlos with theft. They followed the agents who dug up the illegitimate brother of Carlos and set him up in New York as Carlos himself.

They nodded, despite themselves, at the verity of the picture of misgovernment in Berania, the arrest of true republicans, the famine, the misery which came upon the country, and they began to blaze with anger at the persecution of the king who had given up a throne to save his people from bloodshed.

Jervis had not hesitated to place his surmises upon the screen as fact. Thus the audience at the Theatro Libro listened to Torres and his councilors when they decided to murder their own tool, after the victory of Burzio and the royalists, in the hope of quelling the royalist revolt.

And then the scene shifted to Los Angeles, where King Carlos talked with Will Jervis and most reluctantly consented to appear in a film of the story of his life as the only way to convince the people of Berania that he was not dead as they had supposed. And he again declared that he would not try to take his throne by armed force. Only a spontaneous demand by his subjects would recall him.

And there was plenty of excitement in the picture, for the

attempt upon the life of Jervis who had seen Gomez and knew that he was not King Carlos was filmed in detail. And the shot through the window of the transcontinental express was shown and the last effort of the Beranian agents to murder Carl at the Mammoth Studio was vividly portrayed.

The film, however, did not conclude with the magnificent spectacle which had cost Goldsmith so much money. It ended with a scene in which Flores, the captured leader of the Mexican mob, confessed his crimes and laid the blame upon General Torres, then flashed to a closeup of King Carlos in his royal robes and ended with a title in the form of a question.

"My countrymen, now that you know all, what are you going to do about it?"

The answer was a tremendous outburst of cheering and pro-longed cries of "Long live the king!"

AS THE FILM proceeded, it became evident to the Torres adherents who were present that something was being put over on the government. Some of them left their seats and attempt-ed to leave the theater, but were rounded up by the royalists in the lobby and locked in a room in the basement. Others, made discreet by the obvious temper of the audience, sat through the film in silence.

What occurred in Madrova that night happened simultane-ously in a dozen other cities in Berania. And where there was no talking apparatus a silent version was used.

Goldsmith, who had released the picture in America under quite a different title and who laid the story in a mythical kingdom called Sandowa, would have been astounded at the manner in which his masterpiece was being displayed in Berania. The explanation was that he had allowed Will to send a print to the Duke of Burzio via Paris, who, with French motion picture experts, had deftly turned it into royalist pro-paganda.

Ten minutes after the ending of the film, General Torres became aware of what had been perpetrated in his capital, but, by that time, the royalists and their can of film had vanished.

A royalist demonstration broke out in Madrova that night which was quelled with difficulty. In other cities it was not put down at all.

By morning each person present at the performance had told ten others about it and by night a hundred persons for each one who had seen the picture knew that Carlos was alive, loved his people, was guilty of none of the crimes charged against him and would return if Berania really wanted him.

Despite every effort of the police and military, the following night the dozen films in the possession of the royalists were shown in other theaters throughout the country and the following day two army divisions in Sepoia revolted and Burzio placed himself at their head. He avoided a battle, which was not difficult, as Torres was uncertain of the loyalty of the troops he sent against him and every day his army grew in strength.

In the meantime the film was released in the United States under the title: "A King of Men," with the statement that King Carlos of Berania in person played the leading rôle.

The American government, under the circumstances, was forced to issue a statement that an error had been made in identifying Alfonso Gomez as Carlos Aronhof; thaat it was true that King Carlos had made this motion picture, but that he had entered the country illegally and would be requested to depart at once.

The sensation created by the picture is still fresh in the memory of motion picture goers. It placed Goldsmith at the head of producers of energy and imagination and it caused acute discomfort to the dethroned monarch himself, while the progress of the revolt in Berania did not please, but alarmed him. He wanted to marry Dalroa Dawning and he couldn't take such a wife to Madrova.

And to Dalma Dawning, the revelation that her chauffeur was a king was almost overwhelming. While he had no throne, at present, it was far from impossible that some day she would be a queen.

CHAPTER XXIX

THE KING WHO CAME BACK

THE USE TO which his film had been put in Berania was unknown to Carlos and also to Isidore Goldsmith who had supplied the copies sent to the Duke of Burzio upon Will Jervis's assurance that he would be paid the customary royalties for exhibiting them and because Jervis had specified it as a condition for inducing Carlos to release the picture.

In the opinion of King Carlos, he had scuttled nil prospects of being recalled to Madrova by letting the picture go out to the exhibitors. Never would his people forgive him, assuming that they ever learned that he was alive and that it was his royal majesty, and not a picture actor made up to resemble him, who appeared in the film.

Strict censorship of the wires and cables from Berania prevented the world from learning of the astonishing use made of the photoplay, "A King of Men." And the progress of the new royalist revolt was successfully cloaked for a few days until, from various sources, rumors crept out that the Torres government was tottering.

Flores, in jail upon a charge of murder, had withstood the quizzing devices of the Los Angeles police and Secret Service Operative Yates for many hours, but he had finally wilted and signed a detailed confession of the operations in the United States during the past few months of the Beranian secret agents, as a result of which, the American government broke off diplomatic relations with the provisional government at Madrova.

Galbo had made his escape in the airplane in which he and Flores were to have flown to Mexico and, feeling reasonably certain that no further attempts upon their lives were to be expected for a while, King Carlos and Will Jervis moved into a suite at the Ambassador Hotel. Carlos was hard put to resist the determination of Los Angeles to fête him. He refused all invitations and took most of his meals in his quarters with Will.

The two friends were surprised one afternoon when the butler entered their drawing-room and announced that a gentleman named Swasey wanted to see Carl, to "pay his regards."

The king frowned. "His nerve." he said, "is as astounding as his baseness. Tell him I have no wish to see him."

"Just a minute," said Will, rising. "Isn't that the lout who caused so much of your trouble here?"

Carl nodded.

"If you don't mind, Carl," Will said with a grim smile, "I'll deliver your message in person." He stepped out to the entranceway. There, looking pompous and patronizing, stood Junior.

"Mr. Swasey?" Will asked politely.

"That's the name," Junior said importantly. "I thought I'd drop around and congratulate—"

"Ah, yes. Will you step this way, please?" With unnecessary deference Will led the way to a bedroom.

"I say—" Junior began.

"You are the Junior Swasey who caused the arrest of the king on a trumped-up charge?" interrupted Will. It was an accusation rather than a question.

"Why—" stammered Junior. "That was just a little joke—" He began to back away from the grim-faced Will.

"It was also a little joke when you hired thugs to beat him up, was it? You like your little jokes, don't you, Mr. Swasey? Well, here's one that's going to make you laugh and laugh."

Will was taking off his coat. "You're much heavier than I, so nobody can say it wasn't a fair fight—"

When the house detective and three frightened bellboys finally forced the door of that bedroom, after several guests had complained that a man was being murdered in the room, they found no murder. Instead, they were nearly bowled over by a howling, corpulent figure, blood streaming from his nose, who darted out the door and scampered down the hall, shouting threats of vengeance as he went.

"Let him go," Will said calmly as he slipped on his coat. "He's just overcome with laughter at a little joke."

"That reminds me," said Carl thoughtfully, with a half smile at Will's bruised knuckles. "If it should so happen that I ever return to Berania I must see that Miss Gladys Swasey is invited to be presented at court. Her heart is as good as her brother's is bad."

THE MACHINATIONS of Will Jervis were totally unknown to Carlos or their friendship would have fractured ere this. The American's apparently empty boast in the cafeteria had been forgotten by the monarch.

Just ten days after the forcible showing in Beranian theaters of the film, "A King Who Loved His People," and while the two young couples were sitting at lunch in the living room of the royal suite at the Ambassador, a cablegram was delivered to Will Jervis. His eyes were shining as he waved the message at the king.

"Permit me to be the first to congratulate you upon your restoration, your majesty," he exclaimed.

"Don't talk rubbish. Congratulate me upon my marriage one week from to-day to the loveliest young woman in the universe," replied Carl, drawing Dalma to him.

"Listen to this," said Will.

> Mob stormed the palace this morning. Torres and his associates fled to Paris by airplane. New provisional government

being formed under my direction. Request his majesty to return at once to his kingdom.

    BURZIO.

King Carlos grew deadly pale.

Dalma grasped his hand. "My king," she exclaimed. "Oh, Carlos, I shall be a queen."

"Darling," he replied gently. "According to the law of Berania, no ruler can marry a woman not of royal blood. So I am refusing this damn kingdom."

"But they have had a republic," protested Dalma. "Suppose we were already married?"

"It wouldn't be considered a marriage in Berania, dear. That's why we are going to remain in California."

"Listen, Carl," urged Will. "Burzio's government won't live a month unless you go to Madrova. You are the only possible king. You can't throw your people down for any reason in the world."

"Can't I? Watch me," replied King Carlos of Berania. "Our wedding takes place as arranged."

"You have to be King of Berania to prevent your wife and mine from becoming widows. Lose this chance and in comes another gang of scoundrels who will begin the pursuit of us where Torres left off."

"I am adamant," replied Carlos with dignity. "I love Dalma. That's all that matters."

WILL LAUGHED. "Oh, well," he said, "marry the girl and still be king of Berania."

"I have told you that was impossible."

"Carl," said Will, approaching and taking Dalma's hand, "permit me to present the Grand Duchess Catherine of Russia."

"This is no time for jesting, sir," replied Carl angrily.

"I *am* Russian and my name is Catherine," replied Dalma. "But I'm not a duchess."

"I knew she was a Slav the first time I set eyes on her," stated

Will. "I knew the ring she was wearing because, ten years ago when I was a kid in Washington, I saw it on the finger of the Grand Duke Borislav, her uncle. I didn't say anything at the time because I didn't know how she came by it, but I set detectives to work. Your family, princess, was hated more by the Bolshevists than any other branch of the Romanoffs and for years after the revolution they were hunted down. Your father, Borislav's brother Alexander, changed his name and dropped his rank when he brought you to America fifteen years ago. Borislav was assassinated in New York and Alexander was at his bedside and inherited the empty title and a few possessions left to him.

"He died mysteriously six months later. Your mother fled with you to Chicago, married a man named Joseph Grady and was careful not to tell him anything of her antecedents. That's why you don't know that you're a grand duchess. Carlos, would Berania object to having a princess of the royal blood of Russia as its queen?"

"*Gloria in excelsis!* I should say not," exclaimed Carl. "Dalma, dearest, was there ever a more wonderful romance? You found your king in a chauffeur's livery. I found my queen in a little motion picture actress."

"You can get to New York in two days by plane," said the businesslike Jervis. "In nine days you can be in Madrova."

"The greatest romance in all history!" reiterated the king.

"I debate that," replied Will. "Here is a Beranian spy, a young woman who was set upon me by my enemies, who robbed my luggage and stole from me the Lion of Berania, but she couldn't resist my charms, so she betrayed her associates, enabled us to smash the conspiracy and she is going to marry me and be a good girl for the rest of her life. Aren't you, Aimee?"

"On condition that you don't take me to Berania," Aimee replied smiling. "I do not think the climate will be good for me."

"Well," said Will, "I overthrew the Torres government by

long distance from Los Angeles, for no other reason than to make the world safe for you and Will Jervis."

"You overthrew Torres?" questioned Carl incredulously.

"Now that you aren't going to murder me for doing it," replied Jervis, grinning, "I'll take a couple of hours to tell you how it all came about."

ABOUT THE AUTHOR

FRED MacISAAC IS so well known that *Argosy* readers will be surprised to learn that his first story was published as recently as November, 1924. It was a two-part serial entitled "Nothing but Money."

Previous to that time he had been a musical and dramatic critic upon New York and Boston newspapers, occupying an editorial chair after long years as a reporter and much knocking about the world. He brought to story writing a vast fund of personal experience and an enormous acquaintance among people of every walk in life. He was chummy with sea captains and grand opera singers, longshoremen and college professors, policemen and actors. He was a newspaper man in the days when the editorial room, not the counting room, was paramount. He made excursions into the field of press agenting. Once he traveled all over South America booking a tour for the Russian Ballet and transacted business in the Spanish tongue, which he learned during the sea trip between New York and Lima, Peru, and practiced upon the best people in Latin America.

As a concert manager and producer of open-air spectacles he was famous in New England. He once put on *Aida* in the open air, with two thousand people and a group of Metropolitan Opera stars in the cast, a ballet of a hundred, a stage band of fifty and an orchestra of one hundred, and twenty-five. He discovered a number of singers who have since climbed to

the highest pinnacle of their art. While
he was under the spell of music he followed opera all over the world, and
heard it in Beirut, Milan, Paris, Vienna
and Buenos Aires.

The film business is no mystery to
him. He spent a year behind the scenes
in the biggest studio in Hollywood,
and says he prefers to write for magazines. He likes California and spends
about half the year out where the palm

Fred MacIsaac

trees rustle in the hot air provided by the Los Angeles boosters.

Many of his characters are lifted bodily out of life, which is
the reason they seem so real to *Argosy* readers. Many of the
incidents described in his stories are personal experiences. With
all this background, he still considers himself a young man, and
thinks the world is a very fine place.

Since fiction writing has emancipated him from the daily
grind he roams all over the globe. Manuscripts drift in from
Cairo, Central America or Hawaii, and every now and then he
walks into the *Argosy* office and is annoyed to find the editor
has an engagement for lunch.

THE ARGOSY LIBRARY ™

SERIES 2 INCLUDES:

* BRAND * BRENT * ADAMS *
* MacISAAC * ROSCOE *
* GIESY & SMITH *
* BECHDOLDT *
* MONTGOMERY *
* FARLEY *
* DAVIS *

THE BEST FICTION
FROM THE FRANK
A. MUNSEY LINE

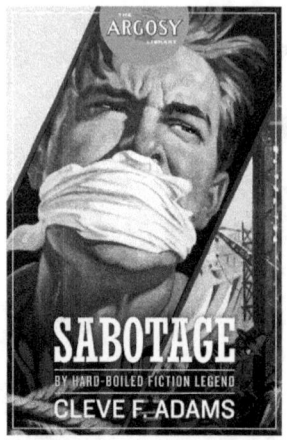

SABOTAGE
BY HARD-BOILED FICTION LEGEND
CLEVE F. ADAMS

CHAMPION OF LOST CAUSES
MAX BRAND

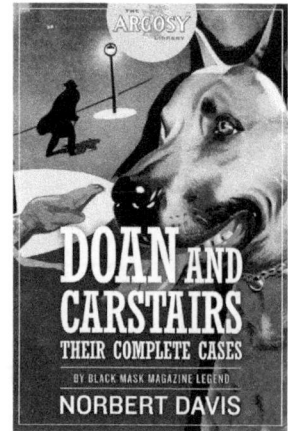

DOAN AND CARSTAIRS
THEIR COMPLETE CASES
BY BLACK MASK MAGAZINE LEGEND
NORBERT DAVIS

THE KING WHO CAME BACK
BY THE AUTHOR OF THE RAMBLER
FRED MacISAAC

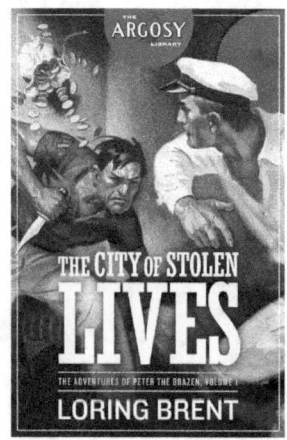

THE CITY OF STOLEN LIVES
THE ADVENTURES OF PETER THE BRAZEN, VOLUME I
LORING BRENT

THE RADIO GUN-RUNNERS
BY SCIENCE FICTION LEGEND
RALPH MILNE FARLEY

BLOOD RITUAL
THE ADVENTURES OF SCARLET AND BRADSHAW, VOLUME I
THEODORE ROSCOE

THE SCARLET BLADE
THE RAKEHELLY ADVENTURES OF CLEVE AND D'ENTREVILLE, VOLUME I
MURRAY R. MONTGOMERY

THE COMPLETE CABALISTIC CASES OF
SEMI DUAL
THE OCCULT DETECTOR, VOLUME 2: 1912–13
J.U. GIESY AND JUNIUS B. SMITH

SOUTH OF FIFTY-THREE
BY THE AUTHOR OF THE TORCH
JACK BECHDOLT

SERIES 2 • AVAILABLE SPRING 2015

www.ingramcontent.com/pod-product-compliance
Lightning Source LLC
Chambersburg PA
CBHW071838020726
47502CB00004B/1416